THE BILLIONAIRE MOB WIFE
LOVING THE BAD BOY

A Complete Novel By
CHRISTINE GRAY

This is a work of fiction. Names, characters, businesses, places,
events and incidents are either the products of the author's
imagination or used in a fictitious manner. Any resemblance to
actual persons, living or dead, or actual events is purely
coincidental.

Contains explicit language & adult themes suitable for ages 16+

Remember….

You haven't read 'til you've read #Royalty

Check us out at

www.royaltypublishinghouse.com

Royalty drops #dopebooks

<u>Other stories by This Author under the name</u>
<u>SAPPHIRE</u>

Don't Tell My Husband Series

Falling for an Alpha Billionaire Series

Consumed by Love

An Extraordinary Love; The Angie n Levi Story

One of a Kind Love; A Seasonal Romance

Dear Readers,

Yes, I'm at it once again. This story, I've been told is a bit different from the others that I have penned, but I promise you that this is NOT a new trend.

As a writer, I have to explore new ways of entertaining you, and making you fall in love. If I didn't, I don't think you all would stick around for the same fried chicken and toss salad, right? So, rest assured that even through my pen name has changed from <u>SAPPHIRE (ROSE)</u> to <u>CHRISTINE GRAY</u>, I'm still the same old person that writes the stories you love that have humor, drama, crazy twists, mouthwatering alpha males, romance, and knee jerking, back popping, good to the last drop, sex!!

Ok, so enough talk. I hope U enjoy the ride! Please, leave a review.

Till Later PEEPS...

CHRISTINE GRAY

CHAPTER 1

Two years earlier...

"I tell you that ref is blind as a fucking bat. I could do a better job than him," mumbled Calico as she slumped down into the light blue stadium seat.

Andreas chuckled. It was only ten minutes into the Miami Heat versus Cleveland Cavaliers game and he could see that it was going to be an interesting night. He was happy he had listened to his boys to come out to the basketball game. He thought it was going to be the same old thing: beer, and shallow females that tagged along all in hopes of getting "the hook up." Most of them didn't even know a thing about the players or the game. They were just present for the good time and to be seen. Many of the chicks were friends of his boys, cousins, or sisters. It was nothing for these men to use these opportunities as a chance to climb up the social ladder if one was willing to take the bait. He had come to the game that night thinking that Rush's sister was going to be the same. But, there he was sitting next to this woman in shock that she clearly didn't give a damn about him.

He had taken the seat next to her out of politeness, because Rush had begged him to do so the entire day at work. The fact that she looked fine didn't hurt, but that did not stop the churning in his stomach as he made his way down the row to his seat. If she was anything like her kiss ass, motor mouth brother, he had already thought up a reason to exchange his seat with someone else. However, when he settled into his chair, the fact that she hadn't made an attempt to engage him in conversation was strange. Instead, she quietly observed and listened to everyone around her. Him being so close to her, he was able to hear the light smirking she did at the antics of the other woman. Or a few times, he was gifted with a word or two she mumbled under her breath. All the while, she continued to sit with a bright smile painted on her full lips and never letting on to her true thoughts.

Glancing away to pretend to look at something on his phone, Andreas tried to think of a way to trick her into talking to him. For some reason, she baffled him. Why wasn't she trying to get him to notice her? If she wasn't there for that reason, then why the hell did Rush plead for her to be put on the list to attend the game?

"I wish that damn girl would sit the hell down and shut up," he whispered as he shifted in his seat, leaning closer to her while he stared into his phone.

"What? If she wasn't laughing, then you might not think that your jokes were actually funny," replied Calico with a smirk.

The blank expression he gave her was priceless. She had to turn away to keep from bursting into a fit of laughter. Andreas's deep blue eyes scanned her with a new intensity. Her response was not what he expected. But now that he had gotten her to finally acknowledge him, he was determined to feed his curiosity.

"Are you implying that I'm not funny?" He waited for her to look back at him. When she did, he found himself caught by the look, or better yet, the color of her eyes. He hadn't noticed until then that they were gray. It was a strange feature for her to have with her skin tone being the color of dark chocolate. It made him wonder if they were real. He leaned oddly forward to get a closer look.

"Is there something on my face?"

"Oh, no. Your eyes, I was trying to see if they were contacts."

"So, what else on me do you want to know if it's fake?" She frowned as his gaze traveled to her hair, then to her breasts, then finally, he leaned back to make a big show of trying to look at her ass.

"Well, I can tell that your ass is real. As for the breasts," his hands went to his chest, "I don't think *Victoria's Secret* make bras with that much padding, so I'm guessing those are real, too."

"Oh, you'll be surprised at the things you can get from that place. I could take this off and be as flat chested as that chick down there," she nodded with her head to the mixed girl that was talking to one of his friends.

Andreas followed her gesture and made a sickly sound which caused them both to laugh. "I think he should check her license just to make sure she really is a girl before he gets the surprise of a lifetime," he chuckled.

"As for the other things on your list, my hair and eyes are both real. I can't blame you from wondering. I get that question all the time about my hair and eyes, but not my ass and breasts," she added when his eyebrow went up.

"Well, you can't blame a man for asking. I just want to know what I'm getting myself into."

Calico's eyes scanned his face. The man was handsome as hell. It was obvious that he knew it and all the women around them knew it, too. She had already gotten a few nasty stares her way because he had chosen to talk to her instead of them. It wasn't as if she had asked for him to sit next to her, let alone talk to her. She found it much more enjoyable to watch the women make fools of themselves while trying to get his attention.

"You're planning on getting into something tonight?" she asked in a low voice.

Andreas felt his dick leap to life from the tone of her voice and her play on words.

"That is the plan."

"Then I suggest you concentrate your energy on one of the girls in the group. For some reason, I think I would be very disappointed," she said as she glanced at his crotch before she turned to the court below. She wouldn't dare look back at him. The fact that he had chosen to sit by her was all the confirmation she had needed that he must have been the 'important friend' her brother briefed her on at home. She smiled, nodded, and agreed to everything her brother said to her at home and all the way to the stadium.

This can mean big things for me, Calico. My friend has a lot of pull, and he could help me move into some really big places," he repeated. "*I told him that I was bringing you, but the other guys are bringing a girl too so....*" *His words had trailed off when she had walked out of her bedroom into the living room of the small apartment they shared.*

"*You aren't wearing that, are you?*" he moaned.

"*It's a game, Rush, not a club. I'm going to be jumping up and stuff. Heels and a tight dress would be out of place there,*" she pointed out. She could see that her comment made sense to him.

"*Yeah, you right. That would look like you're trying too hard,*" he nodded, but the frown still creased his face. "*What about a different shirt. I mean it's tight, but what about one that showed more of your tits? And not pants, although they're tight, maybe some shorts to show more of that ass of yours," he suggested.*

She had wanted to tell him to kiss her ass, but she didn't. She did what she always did which was smile, nod, and keep her comments to herself. It was better that way, she would remind herself, if she just shut up and went along. Five minutes later she returned, this time in a pair of dark green linen shorts. She held her hand up to warn him to keep his mouth closed when his eyes went to her black ankle boots. With a shrug, he changed the subject back to how important it was for her to do him right tonight by giving his friend a try.

Now, she knew that this must be the 'friend' her brother was pushing her on.

Well, you can bend over and take one for the team Rush, for once," she thought, a bit annoyed.

She figured that he had pointed her out to the guy after he had arrived, and that was the reason the asshole felt he could spit his game to her. Calico was sure that if she ignored him long enough, he would more than likely shift his attention to one of the very eager girls that were in the group. He could spend his time on one of their fake asses. Hell, the only reason why she had jumped at the game was the opportunity to see LeBron in action against the team he had abandoned to win a title. She could care less about Rush. He was always looking for the easy way to obtain what others actually worked and strived to get. She giggled as she recalled something her grandmother had said about Rush one day when she had gotten mad.

"It's a good thing he was born a boy, cuz his lazy ass would have fifty kids to make sure he didn't have to actually work," the old lady said.

Calico cast a quick glance down the row and locked eyes with her brother. He gave her the thumbs up before she smiled and turned back.

Andreas had seen the quick message between the two siblings. What Rush had failed to see because of the distance between them was the eye roll she had waited to do out of his sight as she turned away.

"I bet you do a lot of things behind your brother's back," he teased. This time, she was the one with the shocked expression on her face. She wished he wouldn't have seen that exchange.

"Don't worry. I won't tell your secret."

"Let me guess, for a favor?" asked Calico as she licked her lips. He followed her tongue as it glided slowly over her shiny, red top lip.

He had wanted to say, *hell yes*, but he knew that that would be playing into her hands. She wasn't like the other women. She actually had a brain, and her interest in him wasn't for money or popularity. She was offering him a challenge that he hadn't had in a very long time.

"You need to practice that a bit more in the mirror," he pointed to her lips. "Because if you're trying to look sexy, it didn't work."

Calico tossed back her head and laughed. "Maybe you can play the clown after all," she said, tapping his arm.

Her touch sent a shock wave of lust thundering through his core to his cock.

And you can play the bitch, the voice in his mind screamed.

When the lights went out and the announcer took center court to call out the start of the game, Andreas took that time to watch her. Her brown face lit up with excitement as she added her voice to all the screams that were going up in the stadium. He continued to sit in his chair when she chose to get to her feet to get a better view of the players. His blue eye turned darker for the lust he experienced as he feasted upon her shape. In those tight, short shorts she had on, he was gifted with a clear image of her nice, round ass, and firm thighs. His eyes moved upward to take in her thin waist, toned arms, and when he closed his eyes to gain control of his desire, he was able to conjure up the vision of her large breasts that were too big for a body her size. She was perfect. It was as if God had drawn her blueprint to perfection before he sat down to fashion her in flesh and bone. Obviously, he was having one hell of a day because he chose to also give her almond shaped, gray eyes, full lips, and thick hair which was now piled up on her head to create a messy bun.

The command of the announcer asking everyone to get to their feet for the National Anthem saved him from all of the lustful, immoral thoughts that he was having, involving him spreading her brown thighs wide before he proceeded to fuck her until he had her speaking in tongues.

Calico glanced up into his handsome tanned face at the sound of his deep voice. She was surprised that he could sing that nice, and her expression clearly said so. She was happy that he didn't notice that she had looked his way before she turned back. She had to admit that the man was fine. His natural tanned skin, closely trimmed beard and goatee that framed full, sexy lips along with piercing blue eyes and fashionably cut jet black hair, made a striking combination. She found herself wondering if he always let it hang naturally into his face—the top was longer than the sides and back or if when he was at work, he put product in it to force it to stay in place atop his head. Either way, it still created a very handsome picture.

"Are you planning on watching the entire game standing up?"

Startled, she felt him tug on her hand in an attempt to get her to sit back down. She had been so deep in thought that she hadn't realized the anthem had ended. Nervously, she took her seat, making sure she didn't give away the nature of her true thoughts.

I may have to take this man up on his offer. It has been awhile, she considered.

She crossed her legs as if the screams, and pleading of her pussy could actually be heard. Mentally, she thanked God that she had broken down a few days ago and tamed the bush that had sprouted between her thighs. It wasn't as if she didn't want a man in her life. It was just that she didn't care for the ones she seemed to attract. They were either soft men that offered no excitement at all, or a mirror image of her brother that wanted a woman to take care of them, because they were too lazy to do it themselves. She had been cleaning up after her older brother, and carrying him to the point that she had no desire to have another man that would only work her nerves. Oh, then there were the ones that never asked her views on any topic or what she wanted, because they didn't have a desire to know. She was a safe bet for all those types of men. She offered them beauty, sex, money, and comfort.

Well he, Mr. Tall Dark & Fuckable, could offer you a sore pussy, stiff muscles, and one hell of an orgasm.

She shook her head to clear her thoughts while the tip off below started the game. Thankfully, with that going on, she didn't have the time to think about the man that was sitting next to her. It was only when her hand or her leg brushed up against him was she reminded of his presence.

"Oh my Lord," she moaned in frustration as she cast her eyes heavenward. "How the hell is the ref going to foul the team, but then turn around and give the damn ball over to them?" she stated as she elbowed him in the ribs, forgetting herself. Horrified, she touched his shoulder. "I'm so sorry."

Andreas smiled down into her wide, gray, almond shaped eyes. "You really came to watch the game," he said more as a statement, than a question.

"What other reason would there be?"

Andreas sucked and then bit on his bottom lip.

Ugh, his mouth...those lips, that bottom lip is bigger than the top.

He noticed the way she stared at his mouth. That's when he knew that she wasn't as cold toward him as she had put on. Choosing to not make his thoughts so transparent, his mind worked quickly to come up with a fitting response. From what he had witnessed thus far, he craved to see more of the person that was lurking just below the surface So, he took a gamble on appealing to her obvious love for the game. Fortunately for him, his bet paid off. For the next twenty-four minutes, they laughed, shared strategies, trashed talked, fussed and cursed. It took no time at all for her to warm up to him, or for him to realize she was a one of a kind woman.

"Do you think LeBron's going to leave the *Heat*?" he questioned, not wanting the conversation to end.

Calico did a double take. She had many views on the matter, but no one had ever given her the chance to express them until now. Most people didn't consider her to be a sports' lover. She hesitated for a second before she went to her normal response, which was a smile and a shrug of her shoulder.

"Don't pull that bullshit with me," he grumbled. "I can tell by that look in your eyes that you have an opinion. I really want to hear it," he added. It bothered him that she had pulled that crap on him. He also found himself a bit surprised that he really did want to hear what she had to say.

"Well, um..." she started slowly with her eyes darting back and forth between Andreas and Rush, watching them down the row.

"Why are you looking at your brother?" he asked as he narrowed his gaze. He didn't need to follow her line of vision to see who or what she was looking at.

She debated telling him a lie, but chose not to. "I was warned not to sound too smart. Apparently, Rush thought you wouldn't find that to be a glowing attribute," she smirked.

"Rush is, he's..." he let his words trail off. He didn't want to say something to offend her. He was aware that siblings took no issue calling each other names, but were ready to throw hands if someone else disrespected them.

"You don't have to say it," she chuckled.

He was overjoyed that she had touched him. That was at least the tenth time she had done so already.

"Let me buy you a drink," he offered, hoping a few would loosen her and her thighs up.

Calico's perfectly arched eyebrow went up as she worked her mouth a few times before she answered.

"Tell you what, I'll let you buy the first round, then it's my turn."

Once again, her answered proved that she was completely different from the women that circulated around him like lunatic gold diggers. Andreas turned around to get the attention of the nearby vendor, but came face to face with Rush instead.

"We're taking off," he informed them.

"But it's just half time," cried Calico, sadly. Andreas heard her sigh as she reached down to grab her purse.

"The girls aren't into the game, so we're going to hit a few clubs," Rush explained.

"Then why the fuck did they come?" she mumbled.

Although he was annoyed that Calico was going to give up watching the second half of the game because of her dumbass brother, he was excited about the sudden turn of events. He placed his hand on her lap to signal for her to remain seated.

"You guys go on ahead. We're staying to finish the game."

It sounded more like an order than an offer. Rush didn't even consult Calico to see if she was alright with staying. Her brother turned and walked back to the group of people that had already left their seats and were waiting for him in the walkway to leave. Andreas frowned and shook his head in disgust.

"They only came to be seen or in hopes of seeing someone famous. It's a fucking waste of money."

"Thankfully, it's not yours," she replied as she took the cold bottle of beer from his hands. She briefly took her eye off him to open the beer bottle which kept her from noticing his mischievous expression. He had assumed Rush had told her who he was, but it became very clear that she was in the dark.

"I know right," he joined in with a high pitched voice that made him sound like a gossiping hood girl.

"He paid for all those tickets at what, one twenty-five a pop, and he didn't even show up. He just threw his money away," she continued on.

"Shit, he could have given us that money," he huffed with a deep eye roll. "Hey, if you were strapped like that asshole, what would you do?"

"I'm not even talking being rich like him. All I need is a little bit to get my interior decorating business going."

Andreas was tempted to ask her more about that dream, but he was having too much fun watching her hang herself.

"Well, you know how it is. It's always the wrong people that have the money. So, you've never seen Rush's boss?"

Calico shook her head as she took a drink from the bottle. "No, but he wants me to."

"Why you made an ugly face like that?"

"I just know he wants me to meet him cuz he's hoping for a hookup. Like I'm going to fuck some pot belly whose dick I'd have to search for just so he can get a bonus, ugh," she explained in a disgusted tone.

"Damn, I work hard on those ads, and I promise you—"

His words were interrupted by her uncontrollable coughing. She had inhaled her beer when it dawned on her what he was saying. Her gray eyes grew three times their size as she fought to clear her airway. Holding up her hand, she signaled for him to stop beating her back so hard. Luckily, "The Hills" from the Weekend that was blaring through the stadium during the halftime show, helped to drown out her distress.

Snatching the bottle from her hand, he placed it next to his on the concrete ground, took her shoulders, and commanded for her to breathe deeply. He stared into her water filled, red eyes. After a few breaths, she calmed down, but she wouldn't look at him.

"I'll call a cab and—"

"What the hell for?" he snapped. "You're going to rob me of watching the game with someone that actually wants to be here, and knows what's going on?"

"I'm so sorry," she stated in a hoarse voice. "I thought you were the friend that Rush was trying to get me to 'show a good time'," she explained with air quotes and all.

"Well, we both know how Rush tends to stretch the truth, and how he tells a little, but keeps a lot."

"You're actually very good looking," she blurted out, embarrassing herself even more. She put her hand over her face only for him to pull it away so he could smile into her face.

"Don't treat me the same way you treated those assholes that just left. If you want to make it up to me, let me take you to dinner after the game's over," he suggested.

"Why?"

He shrugged, "Because I want don't want the night to end. I want to see more of that person you keep hidden. I can tell that you're really good at faking a lot of things. But, I am hoping that you don't fake everything," he finished in a deep voice that seemed to reach out and stroke her. The same tight, throbbing feeling she had experienced before in her pussy returned.

"It's up to you to make sure I don't have to," she replied in a husky voice, this time choosing to speak her mind concerning him. She watched as his eyes became hooded, but not before she saw a spark of lust in their blue pools.

"Listen," he began while he placed his warm hand on her inner thigh. "If you give me the pleasure of tasting and feeling you tonight, I want it to be what *you* want."

Calico went still as she processed his words. If she didn't know better, she would have thought that someone had coached him in the right things to say to make her want him. However, she knew that wasn't true. The only person that would have been able to accomplish that would have been Rush, and he had his head so far up his own ass, he didn't have a clue about what she thought or felt. With a smirk, she leaned over and kissed him. Andreas opened his mouth to meet hers. He wanted to remain still and just enjoy it, but he couldn't. On contact, the heat that was on a low shimmer instantly became a flame. The way she moved her tongue to caress his mouth, the feel of her soft lips, even the taste of the beer on her, all combined to cause him to act impulsively. Quickly, he lifted her up and placed her on his lap. His hand went up to capture her head and pulled her closer. It must have been the sound of the loud buzzer bringing the half-time to an end that broke the trance.

"I can see I won't have to search for it after all," she mumbled against his lips. Her eyebrow went up when she felt his dick jump under her ass. Slowly, she got up and went back to her seat next to his to focus on the last two quarters.

At that moment, Andreas could give a damn if the *Heat* won, he was ready for the game to end. If she fucked half as good as she kissed and teased, he didn't know if he would ever get out of her pussy. Taking a deep breath, he ran his hand through his hair as he told himself to get control. He had been sleeping around since he was a teenager with young, as well as older women that he met through his grandmother. It wasn't as if Calico was going to be his first. By the time the game was over, he was more himself.

As they began the slow trek from their seats to the aisle and ultimately to the upper level to the leave the crowded stadium, she threw her name over her shoulder, "Calico."

"Andreas."

"Ah, so the tan is natural."

Just like that ass, he thought, placing his hand on her waist. He intentionally stopped close behind her. His strong arm snaked around her waist to draw her back against him. She closed her eyes. She could feel his chiseled body against hers. She took a deep breath, which caused her to become temporarily light headed from the smell of his cologne and natural scent.

Once they reached the center aisle, he took hold of her hand. He kept the conversation light and funny as they walked. Even when the crush of people had thinned out, he still chose to hold her hand.

"How old are you? How did you get your business, anyway?" she questioned.

"My grandmother had gotten too old to deal with it, so she gave it to me. I think it's her way for me to prove to her business partners that I can do it, and let me get my feet wet. I'm twenty-eight," he smirked.

"Hmmm, well, that's a blessing to get a leg up."

Andreas chuckled. Her words didn't conjure up the leg she was referring to. He opened the car door to his white Range Rover, and stepped aside for her to get in. Calico slid into the polished leather seats. Nervously, her eyes followed him as he walked slowly back to his side of the SUV. She was happy that he had paused to look at a text on his phone. She leaned forward in her seat to get a better view of him through the door's mirror.

She had to admit that he had an amazing shape. He was tall and fit. He was a nice mixture of lean and muscle. He could easily be one of the men that she liked to pin to her *Pinterest* board. Her eyes locked on his ass when he turned to the side as he typed a message into his cell. She was happy that he had an ass to hold on to. It fit nicely in his distressed jeans that hung low on his hips. With his head lowered, his ink black hair fell over his forehead and into his eyes. She smiled when he subconsciously brushed the locs out of his face.

"I hope you aren't starving, because I have to make a quick stop. I need to pick up an accounting book for my Grandma," he explained.

Forty-five minutes later, he put his SUV into park in front of a towering office building. He noticed how Calico scanned the empty parking lot.

"Are you going to be okay?"

At her quick nod, he hopped out, and looked back at the sound of the vehicle's locks sliding into place. With a sigh, she tossed her head back on the leather headrest as she closed her eyes to think. It was the light tapping on the window that startled her.

"Don't tell me you're getting tired?" he questioned.

She could hear the worry in his voice that she was going to change her mind. His sigh of relief could have blown her over when she shook her head, no.

"So, where do you want to go?" he asked, clicking his seat belt into place. His shock was clearly visible on his face when she took hold of his arm and started to kiss him. It only took him a few heartbeats to catch up with the fevered intensity of her kiss.

He moaned deeply before he broke away from her mouth. He didn't know what had come over her during the time he left her, but he was happy that whatever it was had happened. His mind was already thinking of where he could take her nearby to have sex. Then he warned himself that she might have just wanted a kiss. It didn't mean that she was ready to skip dinner. His blue gaze went to her hand as she pushed the orange colored button to unlock his seat belt.

"What about dinner? I try to be a man of my word," he smiled.

"And I'm trying to be your bitch," she replied huskily.

Quickly, Andreas reached on the left side of his seat, and pushed the lever that lowered the seat back to make room for her. He didn't want food any damn way. Calico maneuvered herself to straddle his hips, facing him.

"I have food at home, but I don't have this," she whispered while she grinded her pussy against his marble hard dick.

"My God," he grunted as he closed his eyes. Her kiss might have been slow, but it was passionate.

This woman can kiss, he acknowledged. His hands traveled just as lazily up her waist, then slid under her shirt. Her body was firm, toned and soft. He needed room. He needed room, now.

"Hold on," he ordered in a strained voice while he pushed her back. Swiftly, he unlocked the doors, slid out of the SUV with her in his arms, and moved her to the large backseat. "Shit," he hissed when her hand took hold of his cock.

No longer caring to play the role of the gentleman, he bucked into her hand. Reaching over, he grabbed her shirt and jerked it over her head.

"Your breasts look so damn good," he said in a deep voice. He narrowed his eyes as he let them free. They looked even better under the light of the full moon. He tested their weight before he lowered his head. He opened his mouth wide to take the entire dark nipple in his mouth to suck hard.

Calico went still at the force of his suckle. It sent electricity straight through her body, causing her juices to soak her panties. He encircled, then flicked the hard bud with the tip of his tongue. Slowly, he lowered her back onto the seat. His touch was light as his hand traveled from her collarbone, down the valley of her breasts, over her taut stomach, to the button of her shorts. His eyes never strayed from hers while as he opened and unzipped them. He didn't have to tell her to lift up to allow him the freedom to remove them. No longer was he in a rush. For some reason, he had a strong desire to slow down. He wanted to make her crazy with desire before he fucked her.

Her heated gaze followed his hand as it moved up her inner thigh. He wasn't even at her cunt yet, but he could feel the heat radiating from it. Under hooded lids, he slipped his finger into her thong.

"You're dripping," he moaned.

His head turned at the sharp intake of her breath. He couldn't look away even if he wanted to. The illumination of the moonlight on her brown skin was almost unworldly. Andreas finger parted the lips of her pussy to find the soft flesh in the center. He didn't know what he expected, but it wasn't the tight, wet, throbbing cunt that Calico willingly offered him as she opened her legs wider to make room for his strong hand. Her loud whimpering echoed throughout the car as she moved her hips in tune with his fingers. Leaning over, he tasted her cries as he slipped another finger into her body while he rubbed his thumb over her swollen clit.

"Can I taste you?"

The sound of a throaty moan was her only reply. She could tell that this wasn't the first time he fucked in his backseat from the quick way he moved between her legs. At that moment, she didn't give a damn. She tilted her head to the side, reached down, and pushed his hair out of his face. She wanted to see him lick her dry.

"Fuck," she cried at the feel of his mouth on her shaved cunt. Gripping his head, she urged him forward as she rose up from the tan leather seat to meet his mouth. Maybe she was out of practice. Maybe it had been too long, but the way he licked, hummed, sucked, and fingered her pussy was unlike anything she had experienced with her other lovers. Andreas knew what he was doing. He knew when to lick lightly. He knew when to drop light kisses on her shaved lips. He knew when to blow, and he knew how to flick and tap on her clit with the tip of his tongue until she came into his mouth.

Sitting up, Calico pushed him back, and straddled him, once again. Andreas chuckled at the way she bobbed up and down on his strong legs like an impatient child while he opened his jeans. His thick cock rested against his ripped abs. This time it was his turn to inhale sharply as she traced a vein from the root of his dick to the mushroomed tip that stopped at least four inches above his belly button. She removed her hand to let him roll the thin plastic down his thick, long cock. Wasting no more time, she leaned up on her knees, positioned herself, and began to slowly lower herself down the length of him. Andreas bit his bottom lip at the feel of her tight pussy giving way to one juicy inch at a time, as he penetrated her body. The pace she was taking was torture, but it was of the sweetest kind. Taking matters into his own hands, he gripped her hips and forced her downward as he thrusted upward to meet her.

Calico swayed forward from the delicious feeling of being filled.

"Are you alright?" he asked as he touched her cheek.

"My God, you're big," she moaned. "That's the spot." She leaned forward as she rotated her hips to draw his thick dick further into her body. He opened his mouth and began to suck on her dark nipple as he reached back to slip his finger into her already stretched pussy. She started slow, but after she was used to the feel of his cock, she picked up the tempo.

"That's my girl," he whispered as he placed his hands to rest on her hips while he shifted his weight. The vehicle began to rock after he took hold of her hips and started to pound her at a rapid pace. He bit down on his bottom lip as he watched her head began to wobble on her shoulders from the fast tempo of his thrusts. He brought her up until just his mushroomed tip was still buried, and then he brought her down hard in one quick movement.

"Fuck, I can feel you in my belly," she cried.

"Well, you're going to feel me in your ass," he grunted. In a blink, he pulled out, pushed her out of his lap, turned her round, and pushed her against the back door. He paused long enough to stabilize his weight on his left knee, which he had pressed into the leather backseat, before he started up again. He knew that it wouldn't be long before she was ready to cum. He arched his back as he took hold of her shoulders so he could pull her back to meet his dick.

Calico loved that popping sound her pussy made when he was really getting up in it. In and out, deeper and harder, he tapped on that spot until her cunt rained down its thick juices all over his cock. She was happy he slowed down so she could enjoy the feel of her walls clenching around him. When he knew she was coming down, he dragged her back off the door, pushed her head down into the seat, as he lifted her hips before he began to move inside her again. She let out a scream of pleasure just seconds before she felt his dick jerk, as it pumped his hot cum into the rubber.

"You just had to pop off another one before I finished," he laughed.

"Thank you," she sang while she stretched.

"I know you weren't faking that," he stated.

"No," she giggled, shoving his arm playfully. "You were great. I was thanking you for the end to a wonderful night."

Andreas's movements slowed to a stop. His eyes narrowed while he watched her put back on her thong and shorts, before she reached over him to grab her shirt and bra off the floor.

Did she just dismiss me? he marveled.

"We still have time for dinner," he offered.

"I would prefer to just go home. Besides, I'm very satisfied," she smiled. Without warning, she opened the door to go back to the front passenger's seat.

Calico kept up a stream of chatter on the ride back to her place, but Andreas didn't really want to talk. He was too busy trying to figure out what the hell just happened?

She beat your ass to the punch, the voice in his head pointed out. Countless number of times he had given a generic excuse to leave after he had completed his task. But to his memory, he had never been on the receiving end.

Why the hell hadn't she considered that maybe I was the one that was hungry? Shit, I did just work up an appetite, he grumbled mentally.

"The turn is at the next road. Right here," she pointed to the ten story apartment building in the Opa-locka District. "Thanks again for the game," she smiled as the Rover coasted to a stop.

"I still would like to take you up on that offer for dinner."

Calico's hand paused on the door handle for a second before she turned to face him.

"I don't really think that's a good idea," she responded with a wrinkled nose. "I mean, you're Rush's boss. I don't want him getting over just because we're seeing each other. He's lazy enough." Quickly, she leaned over, kissed him on the cheek, and hopped out the vehicle.

"Good night, and drive safely," she added in a rush, shutting the door behind her.

Andreas closed his mouth after he saw her disappear into the building.

**

Four days later, Calico opened the door to find the FedEx man standing on the threshold. With a smile, she signed for the large envelope, and kicked the door closed. Her eyes went back to the British murder mystery she had been glued to on Netflix. Her gray eyes darted back and forth between the TV and the letter, as she pulled on the strip to rip it open. Her hand fished in the cardboard until she retrieved, yet another envelope, this one being much smaller. Frustrated she was missing key information of the storyline, she frowned as she opened it until she went deathly still. Her eyes widened as she read the note and realized what was inside the card.

"For your leg up. Pun intended.

Andreas."

Calico blinked to refocus her eyes on the ten thousand dollar check she held in her hand.

CHAPTER 2

Present day

Calico dragged into her apartment building. The long days and even longer nights was starting to take its toll on her. She let out a moan. The strap of her purse was cutting into her shoulder due to all the files she had stuffed into it. She hated bringing work home from the office, but lately, she didn't have a choice. She would have preferred using her nights to work on the designing projects she had coming due. However, her new supervisor seemed to have it out for her. The damn woman would purposely wait 'til the last moment to give her the information she needed to get her work done. It didn't matter that Calico would flood the woman's email with follow up messages inquiring on the files. The boney middle aged lady would come by her desk to drop off a mountain of files, leaving behind the heavy smell of cigarettes in her wake. For the life of her, she couldn't figure out what she had done to piss the bitch off. She came to work on time. She never left her chair unless it was for her break or to use the bathroom. She never pretended to work, but was actually on her phone. She dressed according to dress code even though the other female employees in the accounting department didn't seem to give a damn. She was the model employee.

Of course, the few people in the office she considered friends had told her that was the problem. They said she was too damn good. No one, let alone the supervisor, wants to be outdone by a lower employee. Calico sighed, and thanked God once again that she had her own thing she was working to get off the ground. It had taken her awhile, but it seemed as if things were working in her favor. Maybe, if she played her cards right, she'll be able to march into her supervisor's corner office and tell the bitch to kiss her ass before she threw her resignation on top of her desk.

A big smile formed on her full lips at that thought, as she placed the key into the front door. Unfortunately, the smile turned into a loud scream. A dark figure materialized out of nowhere behind her to press her up against the wooden door.

"Shut your loud mouth. Hurry up and open the damn door," cried the man from behind.

"Rush...Rush, is that you?" she asked as she fumbled with the lock while she tried to get a glimpse of him over her shoulder. She hadn't seen or heard from him in a week.

"Hurry up," he shouted as he shook her, as if doing so would make her move faster. When he heard the door finally give way, he shoved her out of the way to enter the apartment. Stunned, Calico walked in, and kicked the door closed, then turned back to see what was blocking it from closing.

"She's with me," mumbled Rush. He paced in a circle while he waited for the woman that had drove him home to enter the apartment.

Calico eyed the pale red head as she passed by. There was something wrong. It was more than the chill she felt run up her spine that told her that. It was also the fact that Rush was wearing a hoodie. Her brother couldn't stand being hot, but there he was in long sleeves and all with the hood pulled low over his face in the hot swamp called South Florida. The woman quietly sat down in the arm chair, plopped her purse of the floor, crossed her legs, and watched them as if she was awaiting a play to start.

Calico opened her mouth to speak, but was cut off.

"I'm in trouble. I mean some deep, stank, dirty, elephant size shit," he said in a shaky voice.

"I don't have any money. I'll tell you that right now," stated Calico as her gray eyes darted back and forth from her brother then to the waiting redhead.

"Fuck money. That shit isn't gonna help me," he replied. He reached up and pulled off the hood.

"Your face?"

Rush paused for a second to look at his sister as if she was crazy. He was in for far worse than the beating he had received at one of the nightclubs a few days ago. Walking over to stand in front of Calico, he grabbed her shoulders, and lowered his face until it was just inches away from hers. At that closeness, he looked like a brown-skinned crack head to her because of how wide he had opened his eyes to stress his point.

"They're talking about putting me in jail for *life.* Do you understand? *LIFE!!* I can't do jail. I can't be raped, Calico. You have to help me."

She bit down on her lip to keep from screaming out in pain that his boney fingers were creating on her tender flesh.

Shaking loose, she said, "I don't know who you killed, but I'm not helping you hide a body."

"Have you lost your mind? You know I can't stand the sight of blood. No, it's not that," he insured her.

Sasha tapped her French manicured finger on her thigh. She watched the girl closely to see if she would be the key to her mission. Her brother had thrown his sister on the table and said that she would be better for the task that they had tagged him for originally. She didn't know if that was the case, but she was willing to break a few eggs to achieve the goal. The girl and her chicken shit brother were just pawns.

"Let me clear things up for you. It's Calico, right?"

Calico leaned around her brother to get a look at the woman that had been watching them argue.

"First off, my name is Sasha. It's not my real name, but it's the one I've been using for a while, so it's grown on me," she began. She was amazed at the poker face that the girl was able to muster up. Most people would have become frightened already, but the woman just sat calmly, hanging on to her every word. "Your brother was beaten up at a club a few days ago after flashing way too much cash in front of the wrong people."

Calico rolled her eyes and nodded.

"That's when we picked him up."

"*We?* Who exactly is that?" question Calico.

"The D.E.A. We reached out to your brother to help us in an ongoing investigation." Now, that got the reaction she had been expecting. Calico's eyes grew three times their size as she worked her mouth, but nothing seemed to come forth.

"Why is the D.E.A coming after my brother?" *Had Andreas gotten into something illegal? Oh God, maybe he was really a dealer even then. He was really young to have had such a big corporation?*

"Because Rush's employer is actually a big time dealer."

"And he's going to be the inside man that's going to bring down the operation," Calico finished in a high pitched voice. She was a big enough fan of mysteries, and *Law and Order* to know where the woman had been headed. She shook her head sadly as she looked at Rush. "Well, you won't have to worry about jail because you're going to die. You see how frightened he is," she pointed as she glanced back over at the agent. "He's going to die," she stated matter-of-factly.

"I agree. That's why we're here. He suggested that *you* would be much better fit to do the job.

"You fuckin son of a bit—" she spat before she clamped her mouth shut. "I don't know anything," she grunted with her hand up. "I only met the man once over two years ago." The confused look on Sasha's face gave her reason to pause.

Sasha tossed back her head and laughed. Glancing over at Rush, "She has no idea. You never told her," she said. Her brown shocked eyes looked the man up and down. "Calico, you and your brother work for the same man. I'm sure you see him every day."

"I don't work at the warehouse," she mumbled.

"I quit working that job last year," he snapped. "How the hell you thought we got this apartment?"

She sat back to let everything wash over her. Of course, she wasn't going to tell him that she had thought Andreas had given him a promotion after their back seat rump, just like the ten-thousand-dollar gift. Suddenly, she started with a jerk.

"Wait, wait… you said we work for the *same* man. You mean to say Russell is a drug dealer?" she asked in awe. The man was always laughing. He was generous, too. Of course, he did make a habit of sweating the female staff, but Calico had chalked that up to him being a nasty old man doing his best to relive his glory days. Although now that she thought about it, she had caught a few things off with some of the accounts. Worried that she might have been at fault, she had doubled, then tripled check the figures only to come up with the same end result. Being the model employee, she had taken her findings to her supervisor.

Maybe that's the reason the bitch hates me, she considered.

"Are you sure? Never mind," she remarked in her next breath, holding up her hand for Sasha to not answer. "Of course you're sure. You wouldn't be here if you weren't. Damn! And you got me that job knowing all of this," Calico continued to babble. She narrowed her gray eyes to glare at Rush leaning against the wall. She had stopped viewing him through the rose colored glasses of their childhood a long time ago. After their grandmother had died five years ago when she was nineteen and Rush was twenty-three, it had only been the two of them against the world. Even though they had family that could have helped them, no one did. She had dropped out of school and got a job to keep them afloat, since Rush always seemed to be losing his. That was until he started at the warehouse. Then she was able to continue college full time while working full time, too.

She closed her eyes and thought back to her grandmother. That woman had done her best to raise her and Rush, when their father was nowhere to be found. Their mother had just decided one day that she was done with being a parent, left them, and never came back to pick them up. That old woman had seen into Rush's soul a long time ago. She had recognized the crooked, broken, and selfish spirit in him then. In spite of it, she still tried, prayed, and preached in hopes that it would take root, but it seemed that it never did. He blamed everyone for his shortcomings, missed opportunities, and was never willing to put too much effort into anything.

"I don't know anything, but I can copy files and pass them off..." Calico's words trailed off at the sad expression on Sasha's face. She was sure they heard the loud churning of her stomach. Her bowels were preparing to give way under the stress.

"We're not the IRS, hon."

"Then I can't help you."

"Thanks to Rush's gift of throwing others under the bus, he has given us an opportunity that we otherwise wouldn't have come up with. It appears that Russell has been putting a dangerous synthetic drug by the name of *flakka* on the streets. We have enough information to take him down, but we can't until we know who his supplier is."

Calico was proud of herself at how she was able to keep a straight face. She had heard people at work talking about a drug that turned the users into walking zombies with some of them actually turning into man eaters under its effect.

"I must be dumb cuz I'm still not catching on here."

"We have arranged for you to take on a decorating job. It will put you in the right place to see and hear the information that we need."

"But why would—"

"Because he *knows* you. You won't be a threat."

"Do you want me to pack his stuff now?" inquired Calico as she got to her feet. There was no way she was doing this.

"Rush tells me that he has given you money. It that true, Calico?"

She stiffened at the icy tone of the woman's voice. "Of course he did. He pays half of the bills."

"So you've taken drug money *and* you work for the same man that your brother also works for who happens to be a drug dealer," Sasha explained slowly so she could understand her meaning. "It won't paint a pretty picture in court."

"Are you threatening me?" Calico whispered.

"Heavens no. I'm just using my gift to look into your future, that's all," smiled Sasha.

**

Calico was having a hard time staying focused at work. To be honest, since that day two days prior in her apartment, she had fallen from her star rating at her job. When she came into work, she didn't do a damn thing. The stack of files waiting on her to be balanced just sat there on her desk. Every so often, she would snatch one up, open it, and stare at the numbers, only for her to toss it back down a few minutes later. In her mind, what was the use? She was a dead woman walking. She was a lone fish about to swim in a tank of sharks. She had already started researching her life behind prison bars by watching the first season of *Orange is The New Black* on Netflix. The way she felt, maybe she was on that zombie making drug because that's the way she had taken to walking around.

She lifted her head in her cubicle to hear what the girl said on her way by.

"Okay," Calico answered as she got to her feet to shuffle up to the front to see who had come to the office to see her.

I swear if it's Rush, I'm going to do the world a favor and kill his ass, she promised as she tightened her grip on the pen in her hand. She had thrown him out along with Sasha that day. She hadn't heard from him since. She held out her hand, pushed open the glass door, and walked into the lobby. The sun shined brightly as if she wasn't living in hell.

"Someone's here for me?" she asked the receptionist. She followed the platinum blonde's gesture to the man whose back was to her. She frowned while she eyed him from behind. He seemed strangely familiar to her.

"Excuse me. How can I help you?" she asked. Her entire world seemed to switch to slow motion. He turned to face her and she about passed out. She took a step back as if it was Satan before her instead of the man that she had had sweaty sex with two years ago.

"Andreas," she shrieked.

The smile he gave her stole her breath away. Maybe it was the bright sunlight on his tanned skin? Or the way his eyes sparkled? Or the way his tailored suit hung to perfection? Or the fact that he had been the last person she had slept with which caused all the memories of that night to come rushing back. But, he looked even sexier now than he did two years ago. There was a strength about him, a confidence, and something else that he did not possess the last time.

He regarded her from behind his hooded gaze. She looked fine as hell in her form fitting light gray pencil skirt and royal blue silk wrap around shirt. The overlapping material created a deep V that offered him a glimpse of her full breasts. He reached out and pulled her into his embrace. He knew the girl behind the desk was watching them.

"What are you doing here?" Calico stuttered.

"I'm here to take you to lunch. I owe you one, remember?"

"I... I can't leave. I—"

"Sure you can," he commanded while he guided her toward the door.

"But my purse, my phone, I—"

"Leave it," he hissed, dragging her through the doors. He led her to his car, opened the door for her, waited until she got in, and then slipped into the driver's seat. The roar of the sports car coming to life made her jump.

"Do you mind if I smoke?" she asked.

He cut his blue eyes at her before he pushed the button to let the windows down. He leaned forward to push in the cigarette lighter. He watched her reach into her bra and produce a joint.

"Where did you get that from?" he grunted as he switched gears.

"A friend at work. I normally don't smoke, but it's been one hell of a week," she explained.

"Why don't you wait until *after* lunch to partake. I don't want you to be brain dead."

She shrugged, placed it behind her ears, and slumped down in the seat. She looked so depressed.

"I think you're going to like where I'm taking you."

Again, another shrug as she glanced out the window. She closed her eyes and enjoyed the air on her face as he sped down the highway. He tightened his grip on the leather wheel to keep his temper under control. He had always known that her brother was a lazy motherfucker. He didn't want to work. He didn't want to start at the bottom. He had tried to encourage him by giving him responsibility, but it only took Rush one time seeing Russell, and he was hell bent on working for the man. All he saw was the quick money. Andreas didn't give a damn about Rush. It was Calico he was worried about. For the millionth time, he tried to understand how they had gotten to that point. He had been working behind the scenes secretly on a plan that would have yielded the same outcome without Calico getting involved, but for some reason, no one seemed to care.

He pulled up into the valet once he reached their destination. He opened his door and looked over for her to do the same. His heart clenched when he realized she had fallen asleep. Gently he shook her awake.

"We're here," he informed her.

"I'm sorry," she muttered, sheepishly. "I haven't been sleeping the best lately. Where are we?" she asked. She cupped her hand over her eyes to shield them from the blinding sun.

"At *A Fish Called Avalon* on Miami Beach," he answered. His hand snaked around her waist as he pushed her forward.

She surveyed the elegant restaurant that had tables lining the walkway under large umbrellas.

"A table outside? And if you shrug your shoulder one more time, I'm going to beat you," he hissed.

Calico blinked, then laughed as she nodded her approval.

Andreas quickly ordered their drinks to get the waiter away. He kept the conversation light due to the fact that he knew the man would be returning soon. It was after they had looked over the menu he let his intention be made known.

"I thought you weren't ever going to cash my check."

"I had to get over the shock. Thank you, by the way. I didn't think I had done anything that great to have deserved it."

"Well, it was good, but I agree not *that* good. I just wanted to help you get going." He knew his statement was only half true. He hadn't been able to duplicate the experience he had with her with anyone else, and it wasn't because he hadn't tried. God knows he had tried, but to no success.

"Well, I wanted to do right by that, leg up. I did my research. Then when I was sure, I started taking on small jobs. Mostly staging houses, and a few shops."

"You should be given the superwoman title of the year. I don't know how the hell you're going to work and follow your dream plus play undercover agent," he whispered, angrily.

This time, Calico was able to gain control of her coughing after a few seconds.

"Rush told you?" she inquired, looking over her shoulders.

"Oh, I saw him, but didn't talk to him. I beat the shit out of him. I know that's your brother, but he crossed the line getting you involved in this shit."

"Wait, so you know? So it's true then?" she gulped, leaning closer to ensure he didn't have to talk loud. The fact that he had admitted to have roughing up her brother hadn't even moved her.

Andreas sighed, running his hand thru his hair. She was happy he had kept on wearing it the same way.

"Yes, it's true."

"How do—"

"Because I have a few business dealings with him," he answered, quickly. He wanted to stay in control of the conversation to ensure she didn't find out too much until he had gotten what he wanted. He had been up all night plotting this meeting. He was determined for it to go the way he had planned. He almost had her.

"Wow," she remarked in disbelief.

"You have no idea who you're dealing with. Russell is not the man you pass in the hall on the way to the break room, Calico," he warned slowly.

She shook her head as she lowered her gray eyes in defeat. "I don't have a choice. I'm going to his birthday party tonight. Sasha has worked a way for me to do a designing job to get me in to find out the stuff she needs to know."

He saw her shoulders visibly slump. He knew she was right for the picking.

"The job is at his night club. It also the place that he has many of his meeting. Apparently there was an electrical fire that caused major water damage," he kept talking to keep her from asking the question that he saw dancing behind her eyes. *How do you know so much?* "I want to help you. I can keep you safe if you're willing to take my offer."

"I don't want to die," she cried.

"That's not the only danger. Old Russell likes them young. He might not have stepped to you at the office, but he surely will once you step into his world."

Calico shifted in her chair. This was the first life line that anyone had thrown her. She really didn't care what he was offering. In her position, she would have been a fool not to take it. She nodded for him to go on.

"I want you to be my girlfriend while you're undercover."

If the situation wasn't a serious one, Andreas would have laughed at the slack jawed expression of her face. If a strong breeze would have blown in from the ocean, it surely would have knocked her out of her seat and carried her down the street.

"I didn't think the offer was that bad," he laughed, unable to hold it in.

Calico reached for her glass, drained it, then held it up to the waiter for a refill.

"Not bad, just unexpected," she smiled.

It was the first time she had done so in days. It was the first time she didn't feel alone. It was the first time that the crushing burden seemed to have been lightened a bit. No, his offer didn't completely save her from her mission, but it did give her someone she could trust and lean on.

"Thank you," she whispered. "I think I'm going to cry," she warned as she fanned her watery eyes.

Andreas was on his feet and by her side in a matter of seconds. He knew that it was all the emotional stress she had been under taking its toll. He marveled at how fast she was able to gain control before she shed a tear.

"I see you're still pushing her down," he smirked as he gazed down into her face.

It took her a second to realize that he was talking about her knack of hiding her true feelings from people. She started to shrug, then stopped in mid motion at the frown creasing his brow. She tilted her head, "You're different. I don't know what it is, but your sex—"

The sound of the plate hitting the table stopped her. She could see the angry expression on Andreas's face as he flexed his jaw.

"So what do I have to do to be your girlfriend?" she asked attempting to shift the conversation, but the wicked smile on his face brought them right back around.

"You'll have to move in with me. I don't want you to be alone."

She knew what he was saying made sense, but the hot way he said it set off alarms in her head.

"You aren't using this as an excuse to get me... no, of course not," she mumbled as she picked up her fork.

"Why would that thought be so far-fetched for you to believe?" questioned Andreas as he leaned back in his chair. He crossed his strong arms over his broad chest.

"I hope you aren't a cock feeling threatened over the prospect of another poking around in your house. Dear God, I wish I wouldn't have said that now. The thought of Russell, ugh," she remarked as she pushed her food away.

His eyebrow went up at her words. She felt her heart skip a beat at the sight of his dimple in his right cheek when he smiled.

"Is that what you really think? That it's all about the pussy?" He sighed before he spoke again. "If you want the truth, you made me so fuckin' mad that night. I've only told one person this, but the way you dismissed me really got under my skin. You aren't the normal woman that I would spend my time with. I've thought of you often, Calico. Wondered at times if things would have worked out for us if you hadn't been such a damn man about it," he smirked.

"So I pissed you off because I got the jump on the bump," she chuckled.

"But who's to say that would have even happened. I mean, you didn't even let a man get a meal before you kicked me to the curve," he grunted, in mock anger.

"Oh, you ate 'til you were full, if I recall. I'm sorry," she teased as she pretended to soothe him. She leaned over, pulling him towards her as she laughed up into his face. Her laughter died when she caught the look in his blue eyes that he had been hiding behind his hooded lids. It was hot. It was intense. It was primal, and it was all because of her. She backed away slowly. Her gray eyes followed his hand as he moved to caress her cheek.

"I desire to get to know you on a deeper level. I want to know who you really are, because from what I've seen, I find you to be very tempting," he stated in a deep voice.

Andreas could hear the change in her breathing. He inhaled deeply. He could have sworn he could smell her scent, the one that was hers alone being carried on the breeze. He wanted her. Shit, he had never stopped wanting her. She had left a strong imprint on him. Only one other woman in his life had ever managed such a feat. However, he wasn't going to press her. She had been on one hell of an emotional roller coaster today. He wanted to ensure she wanted *him* too. At least, that's what his mind said. However, when she spoke, his body began to scream something completely opposite.

"How deep, Andreas?" she inquired in a low voice.

"Your words, Coco," he replied in a strained voice. He felt a surge of lust run through his core as it sent a rush of blood all the way to the mushroom shaped tip of his dick.

She blinked then smiled at the nickname. No one had ever made her experience the heat or to be more accurate, made her feel drop dead sexy, let alone encouraged her to speak her mind until she had met him. No one ever seemed to care if she blended into the background just as long as they could depend on her to be there in the time of need. He spoke of her making a lasting impression on him. Well, he wasn't the only one. She had admitted to herself a while ago that that he was the reason she had chosen to focus on using the opportunity he had given her instead of wasting her time on dating. She had made up in her mind not settle for less of a man because he had proven that guys that could see beyond her mask were out there.

Yeah, but now the wait is over. He came to you. He's asked you to move in with him, which you damn sure will. Now will he be guarding you in his bed, in the shower, on the floor, in the back seat of that car. No, that car is too small, but maybe—"

"What are you thinking?" he asked. He could tell it was something good from the goofy, crooked grin on her face.

"Nothing," she snapped as she wiggled in her chair, stealing a quick glance his way.

"Don't do that to me. I've waited all this time to see you again." He didn't want her hiding what was on her mind. He wanted to see her, for all she was.

"I was just wondering if this arrangement will be coming with *benefits?*" She dropped her voice when she spoke the last word, slowly, to stress her meaning.

Andreas sat upright in his chair, grasped her hand off the table, and placed it on top of his cock. He heard her sharp intake of breath as he pressed her palm against it. He leaned towards her. His hot hand touched her knee and began leaving a scorching path up her inner thigh as he moved upward. He pinned her with his gaze.

"I fuckin' hope so," he whispered in her ear.

She felt the roughness of his facial hair as he moved to kiss her neck. His deep moan seemed to vibrate through her body as her hand tightened around his throbbing flesh. Calico closed her eyes and tried to remember the feel of his rough cheeks between her legs. She opened her eyes just in time to stare into the face of a condemning older woman as she strolled by on the sidewalk. Quickly, she snatched her hand away while she pushed Andreas back. She shamefully looked around the area to see who else had been watching her.

He chuckled, showing off that dimple again. He couldn't care less about who watched them. However, he didn't want her to appear to be a slut in the eyes of a stranger. That was something that was reserved for him alone. Maybe it was because his goal was completed or the long night he envisioned with Calico that made his hunger return for her full force.

"Are you ready for the party tonight?" he inquired between bites.

"Yes. My dress is being delivered today. I hope it fits," she mumbled as she pushed her hair out of her face to take another bite of food. "You're coming?"

"Of course, I can't miss his birthday party. What color is your dress?"

"I don't know. I gave Sasha three choices, so I have no clue."

"Fine. Then that makes it easy for me. I'll wear black. I'll send a car by to pick you up. Have your things packed so we can leave the party as early as possible," he finished in a rush.

Ten minutes later, her perfectly arched eyebrow rose at the sight his black polished *Aston Martin Vanquish* as it rolled to a stop before her. The price of the expensive sports car registered in her mind for a moment. He wondered if he had given himself away with the car.

"What are you thinking?" he inquired while he tipped the young man.

"I was hoping you still had the Rover," she admitted.

Andreas was relieved. He tossed back his head in laughter. "Don't let the small size fool you. I can work miracles with it," he whispered hotly in her ear.

"Has it shrunk?" she mocked him fearfully.

Andreas pulled her back. He let her feel his hard dick pressed against her ass. "You never have to worry about that happening anytime soon."

Chapter 3

"This can't be right," Calico cried six hours later. She had returned back to work with a renewed vigor after Andreas had dropped her off. She could tell by the stares that her co-workers gave her that the girl at the front desk had told them about her handsome visitor. She figured that they all probably thought that she had gotten some on her break which would explain the change in her mood. She wished she had. With the ride back to the office being filled with a detailed explanation of all the many ways he could fuck her in the small car had her considering leaving work early. However, the guilt of all the work she hadn't done, sitting on her desk made it hard for her to do so. She had made short work of the files in the remaining hours she had left.

Now showered, bags packed, hair and makeup done, she stood in front of the bathroom mirror glaring at the reflection of a dress she had not ordered. In another place, another time, she would have ooohed and ahhed over the knock off, but not now. Not tonight. She tossed the breathtaking gown on the bathroom countertop, marched back into her bedroom, and snatched up the invoice paperwork. It had her information on it, but it wasn't one of her choices. In rage, she crumbled up the paper, tossing it across the room. It was obvious that someone had other things in mind for her. The more and more she thought about it, she was happy that Andreas had shown up. She knew all too well how people talk out of both sides of their mouth. Sasha says that her only job was information gathering. That all she had to do was redesign a night club. However, it was clear that the woman wanted her to use *all* her assets to do so. If she had shown up tonight, wearing that dress all alone, the offer would have been a very loud and clear one to Russell.

Her eyes went to the large clock that was hanging on the wall. She didn't have time to pull something together, as if she had anything fitting for such an event. The car would be there in less than twenty minutes. Reluctantly, she marched back into the bathroom. She grabbed the dress, took a deep breath, and got to work.

**

Calico had experienced a moment of light headedness when she realized that this was it. She was here now. She had seen Miami beachfront houses like this one only in her dreams and in magazines, but never in real life. She couldn't even begin to imagine living in such a place. The lights from the setting sun cast an orange and red hue on the already brightly-colored mustard-painted house. One by one, the expensive cars slowly drove around the big palm tree that was planted in the middle of the driveway and acted as a turnabout in the gold tiled drive. The place had to be over five thousand square feet. She had no idea that her boss was this rich. He drove a nice car, but she would have never thought. Even the company Christmas party was never over the top in any way that made her or the employees think he was this well off. He hid his double life very well, indeed.

She checked her dress one more time in the car, while she waited for it to pull up to the valet. For the last ten minutes, she had been staring at the large mansion in the distance as she tried to calm her nerves, but now the time for calming was over. Her car was the next up. It was time for her to dig deep and switch it on. Like an actress stepping onto stage, when the door opened, she was in character. She placed her hand into the man's and allowed him to guide her out of the car, leaving the dull person that she had always hated sitting on the leather seats. She exited it, just as she had practiced and seen England's royalty do many times on television. But she was no Kate Middleton, and this was not a royal party being held on some English estate, although the house was damn big enough to double as one.

As directed, she had sent a text to Andreas when she was three cars away from the door. It became very clear to her that she didn't belong in this circle of rich, famous, and powerful people when she stepped across the threshold. She straightened the knock off, peekaboo custom Givenchy Haute Couture by Riccardo Tisci adorned with multicolored crystals and stones that Beyoncé had worn to the Met Gala in 2015. Nervously as she smiled at the gawking guests that filled the large entryway, she whispered, "Let the games begin."

Andreas narrowed his gaze. It didn't take the hush whispers of the people in the front of the home to get his attention. He had seen her the second she entered the room. Like a moth to the flame, she was already attracting men to her side. If he had been a reasonable man, he would have excused their desire to want to meet her as they basked in her alluring presence. She looked mouthwatering in the see through gown that hugged all the right places. That dress was made for a figure such as hers, and the singer who wore it. She had taken the time to tame her thick natural hair by putting them into twists before she forced them into the neat bun on the top of her head. However, Andreas had never been considered reasonable when he felt threatened. It was at that those times that his temper took center stage. He would crush anyone that was dumb enough to get in his way. Breaking away from the boring people he had been conversing with, he strolled slowly towards her.

Like the parting of the Red Sea, he appeared. He could read the *Help me!* in her gray eyes. He tapped his left diamond cufflink as he approached. He was finally at a distance that he was able to hear the words of the man. Unlike the others that had zeroed in on her, he had his back toward Andreas, so he was unable to make a getaway in time like the others had.

"If you don't want me to take you outside and fuck you with a rake, I suggest you walk away."

Andreas didn't raise his voice. It was just what he said combined with the chilling look in his blue eyes that caused the man to bow his head in defeat and obey. In the blink of an eye, the person she had seen was replaced with the handsome man from before. It was then that she realized that she really didn't know a damn thing about him other than he was a pro between the sheets. That flip he had just done had her worried, and questioning her decision to go along with his plan.

Better him than forging alone into "no man's land." or you walking into what Agent Sasha was offering. At least this way, you'll be getting something out of the deal, the voice in her head pointed out.

"I see I should have questioned you more about your dress," he smiled. He dropped a light kiss on her lips. He knew that everyone was watching. He also knew that the people here loved to talk. It was only a matter of time before the guests were talking about them.

"This is *not* what I asked for. I see I have more than one pimp," she mumbled hotly at his confused expression. "My puppet master."

"Hmmm," he replied, taking hold of her hand. He wasn't surprised at all. Calico was a disposable means to an end. "Relax and try to have fun. There's no need to worry about what other people want you to do. I'm sorry," he stuttered out of the blue. "My eyes keep looking at your breasts," he sighed. "Just give me a second," he ordered as he stopped in his step.

Puzzled, she stopped to see what he was doing. Even without the flash that some men in the room needed to wear on their fingers, wrists, or around their necks, this man didn't need any of that to have eyes following his every step and movement. His pure alpha nature, and jaw dropping good looks was all he needed. His muscular build stretched and filled out the jacket to perfection. The tailored, creased pants hung low on his hips and firm ass. His black hair was combed back to lay like an obedient child on his head. She noticed that he had gone to the barber and had his beard cut down on his chiseled jaw line to resemble a dark five o'clock shadow which was just the way she liked it. She fought to keep a straight face as she stared into his deep blue gaze.

"You definitely know how to get attention," Andreas spoke in a deep voice, as his eyes moved over her body.

She hadn't noticed she had been holding her breath as he made a slow circle around her. She could feel herself becoming light headed. She wondered if it was because of the way he was making her feel, as if she was the only woman in the entire place that mattered or the lack of oxygen to her brain. By force, she felt the air return back to her lungs and she was able to steady herself once again.

He waited until he had come back around to stand before her to speak. When he did, he was able to utter one word. "Flawless."

**

Russell had stopped listening to all of the ass kissing that had been going on around him to watch Calico with Andreas. The girl stood out among the crowd of fake asses and heads full of high grade drugs. The girl always had appealed to him. However, after a few attempts, he had come to realize that she wasn't going to be tricked into fucking him with a promise of a bonus. He felt a sting of anger and jealously as he gazed upon her and the Italian. Maybe he should have kept trying after all, he considered. The woman that was standing in his home was not the one he saw whenever he was at the office. He took a deep breath and he could almost swear he could smell her sweet scent over the played out women that were packed into his place.

"Excuse me," he said to his guests as he touched his wife, Wanda's elbow. "Did you know that the girl from the office and he were a couple?"

Wanda searched the crowd to find who he was referring to. "It could be the dress," she suggested then changed her mind. There was too much emotion sparking between the two of them to not be a history there. "No, I didn't know, but I'm the one that invited Calico," she explained quickly before she added her opinion to the topic being discussed around them.

His eyes darted quickly until he found the man he was looking for. He gestured with his shiny bald head for the man to come over. He had no doubt that the nosy gentlemen had already known the answer to his question.

"Did they come together?"

There was no need for Chubby to ask who Russell was asking about. "No, he came. Then she followed after him, but he was waiting for her. He made it very clear that she belonged to him. You do know that she is Rush's sister, and he worked for Andreas *before* you, so..." Chubby ended with a shrug.

"Why the hell would Wanda invite her?" spat Russell. He didn't like blurring the lines of his businesses.

"You have to ask her, although I think it really doesn't matter. I'm sure she would have been here no matter what," Chubby pointed.

He could tell that the boss's desire for the girl went beyond pure curiosity. Shit, that's how he always was when there was new tail on the market. The man felt as if it was his right to fuck it first. He didn't care if it was your wife, your daughter, even your mother, if she was young enough. Chubby had to fight to keep a normal face as he watched his boss survey the group of people across the room. He wasn't dumb enough to let his true feelings for the man shine through. Not only was the man one of the five men that ran drugs and weapons in the city, but he was one hell of a big man. Although he was in his sixties, Russell hadn't lost any of his muscle mass. He was powerful in influence as well as in brute strength. Sure all that weight made him slow, but that really didn't matter when all he needed was one good hit to knock your ass out.

Chubby smiled and looked the six foot, dark-skinned man over. He had to admit that Russell knew how to dress in a way that let everyone one know he was the man. The black on black suit was tailored to hang just right over his broad shoulders and cut in a way to flatten his pot belly. It was a standing joke that he could be Rick Ross's twin. He even had the facial hair, but thankfully not as overgrown as the music producer and rapper. However, he was playing with fire if he was thinking about playing in the Italian's backyard. Andreas was not the one to fuck with. Once he locked his jaws on you, that person could just give it up. It wasn't as if the Italian was just another asshole that was waiting for a crumb to fall from Russell's table.

"Go bring them over here," demanded Russell, breaking into Chubby's thoughts.

He smiled as he watched Chubby walk away to do his bidding. He rejoined Wanda and the others while he waited. He had been annoyed being here, but now he couldn't stop flashing his white even smile as he thought about that sweet, young pussy. He laughed at something someone said and caught Wanda's searching gaze.

The change in his attitude was obvious. It was like night and day, and he had no doubt she was trying to rack her brain to figure out the reason. His eyes darted to see Chubby leaning in between the couple to laugh before he gestured for them to follow him. He took note of the fact that Andreas entwined his hand in hers before he fell in step. Russell looked away and returned back to his conversion. He cursed under his breath as he noticed the expression on Wanda's face. A wide smirk formed on her face as she started to put the pieces of the puzzle together behind his change of mood.

"Happy birthday, old man," chuckled Andreas while he held out his hand. He knew Russell hated when he pointed their age difference for multiple reasons.

Russell returned the insult by obviously undressing Calico with his eyes. "I'm speechless, Calico. I'm surprised."

"There was a mix up. I promise you my first choice wouldn't have made anyone speechless," she explained.

"It's not the dress, Coco," whispered Andreas as he kissed her head.

"I didn't know you were dating," remarked Russell, once again choosing to ignore Andreas's presence.

"Any man with eyes can see that. How did you two meet is what I want to know?" inquired Wanda.

"I met her through Rush a time ago at a basketball game. She didn't give me the time of day."

"So, he chose to bait me into talking about Rush's boss, but I didn't know that it was actually him," she laughed.

"Yeah, I think you said that I probably had a pot belly and a small—"

"Don't tell them that," she cried, elbowing him into silence.

Wanda glanced over at Russell, waited until she caught his eye, then dropped her eyes to his belly with a smirk.

"She almost choked to death on her beer when I told her that *I* was his boss. She didn't know a thing about me," Andreas finished as his eyes moved from Chubby on down the line until he stopped at Wanda, both his message and warning very clear.

All the guests around seemed to find the story funny except Russell who chose to stare at the two.

"So, Wanda said that she invited you?" It sounded more like a question instead of an answer.

Calico glanced at the woman, not knowing really what to say. Wanda was always on point and this time was no different. The short, big chested light-skinned woman had chosen to wear a red pantsuit. The jacket was cut with a deep neckline that allowed for the large diamond necklace to take center stage against her barely covered breasts. Even though the woman's bust line and long light brown hair were fake, she had to admit that the man's wife was fit and attractive.

"Like I said, I invited her," she smiled, moving to stand next to her. "What you all didn't know about her is not only is she beautiful and smart, but she's also a very talented interior designer. Rush told me about her starting her own business, so I went by to check out some of her jobs. That's when I decided to hire her to redo the night club."

Russell clamped his mouth down to keep from cursing his wife out in front of the people surrounding them.

"Of course, that means you'll have to take time off from the office to work around the clock to get the place ready. We're losing money every day it's closed. But not only will you make four times your salary after it's all done, this could be a big break for you, girl," she laughed.

Calico graciously received congratulations from the strangers around her as she processed what was happening. Not only was she playing the mole, but she was getting paid big time to do it. Not to mention kick starting her business to boot.

Andreas cleared his voice, "I hope you won't take offence to us leaving early, although I doubt we would be missed. I have another engagement I'm looking forward to seeing to tonight."

The heat in his words were so intense, they all knew what he couldn't wait to "see to" or better yet, get *into*.

"Just make sure you let her sleep, Andreas. I need her to start in the morning," Wanda called out to them as the pair walked away. She had done her part. The rest was up to Calico.

**

Instead of heading to the double doors at the front of the house to leave, he led her to the French doors which opened to the garden. She breathed in the fragrant night air as she fell in step next to him.

"What is this? A light night stroll through the garden before we leave," she teased. The dark water seemed to sparkle with the lights of the stars above.

"Not exactly," he answered. He pointed into the distance.

Calico froze at the sight of the large two-story yacht that was docked at the end of the pier.

"Don't tell me you're afraid of the water," he groaned.

She wasn't afraid. She was just confused and surprised that he had such an expensive toy. Keeping her thoughts to herself, she shook her head no. She took her time walking up the plank onto the chestnut walkway. A young woman in a crisp uniform greeted them before she gave the order to raise the plank and get ready to cast off. Her mind was racing a mile a minute while she attempted to absorb all the things Andreas pointed out or said about the ship. Finally, the tour ended with him showing her to the sprawling master suite. The floor to ceiling French doors had been opened to let the ocean breeze into the room. A table for two was set up on the balcony. Her hand went out to steady herself at the hard lurch the boat made when the engine came to life.

Quickly, she kicked of her shoes to help with her stability on the rocking vessel. He was still chatting while he strolled around in his socked feet. With ease, he slipped out of his black jacket, jerked off his matching tie, opened the first three buttons of his white pressed shirt, and removed his diamond encrusted cufflinks. He paused to stretch his hand out to her.

"Come eat."

"Where are we headed?"

He pushed in her chair and took his seat across from her. "We're going out a bit to sea."

"Making sure I don't leave?"

"I recall how vocal you can be. I wanted you to exercise that freedom," he winked. He took a gulp of his whisky. "Are you going to tell me what's on your mind?" he asked.

"How can you afford all of this?" She noticed how her question caused a shadow to fall upon his face. For a split second, there was pain reflected in his blue eyes before he managed to blink it away.

"My grandmother named me her heir. She left her entire estate to me, including her businesses," he replied softly.

Now she understood the slight change in him. "I guess you made her proud," she smiled, hoping to lighten the mood.

"I hope I did. I haven't been quite the same since she left me," he admitted. Shaking himself, he glanced out across the water. He thought about the stubborn old woman every day. She had lived her life to the fullest until the end. He had demanded, begged, and pleaded for her to continue her treatments, but one day, she had said she had enough. He just wished he had listened to her when she had told him—

The feel of Calico touching his arm brought him back.

"Is that how you feel when I'm lost in my head?" she teased. "Talk to me."

Over dinner he shared with her how he came to live with his grandma.

"So, you actually have brothers and sisters?"

"Yeah, although I don't know how many. My dad is still out there helping to keep the population strong. He's a man that doesn't have to work, so he lives off the trust fund his father left him, but I guess there was something about me because he brought me to see his mom. He knew that he was going to have to provide an heir, so..." his words trailed off.

"But she didn't have to take you. She must have seen something in you. She sounds like one hell of a woman. A real old school Italian."

"She was, believe me. She took no crap. She had no problem smacking me and my cousin, Beau upside our heads," he laughed. He took note of Calico's heavy lids as she sat next to him. He was torn between doing the right thing which would be letting her sleep, and being selfish. Biting his lip, he got to his feet.

Calico's eyes widened at the sudden movement. "Are we going in now?"

"Yes, you look tired," he responded in a thick voice. He hoped his disappointment wasn't evident in his tone.

"Good," she beamed as she jumped to her feet. "I was debating how I should make my move if you were going to keep talking." Andreas's eyes sparkled. "Is that what you were doing? I thought you were falling asleep on me," he chuckled.

"And go to bed without having this." Calico closed the space between them. She boldly rubbed his dick through his pants. His breath escaped his mouth in a hiss. His strong arm snaked around her waist, pulling her forward. He rotated his hips allowing her to feel his hard dick pressing on her stomach. His strong hands cupped her ass, picking her up. Calico closed her eyes and wrapped her legs around his waist. He stayed still as she began to grind her pussy against his body. Andreas watched her from under lust filled, heavy lids. He could feel the heat her cunt was giving off through the material of his black dress pants.

"I have to feel you, Coco," he moaned as he began to walk toward the bed. It had been too long since he last touched and tasted her. She was like a drug to him. If he could crush her up and snort her, he would have. He watched her panting on the edge of the mattress. She was hot. She was ready, and he knew as he got down on his knees to kneel between her open thighs, she would be wet. His blue eyes watched as she pulled up the hem of her dress to reveal her body, until he focused on the item of his desire. He took his time. His hand started at her hosed ankle as it roamed up her calf, to her thigh where the stocking stopped. He closed his eyes when his hand came in contact with her flesh. He lowered his head and kissed the area just above the lace thigh-high. Turning his head, his gaze burned into the apex of her thighs. He hooked a finger under the side of her panties, running his finger over one of her shaved pussy lips before he pulled the material back to feast upon her trembling pink flesh.

Even though his touch was light when he lowered his head and planted a light kiss on her cunt, Calico jumped back as if she had been burned. Andreas was a master in the art of making her lose control. There were so many nights after their first time together long ago, that she had pleasured herself to the memory of him. He smiled against her flesh when he felt the light pressure on the back of his head as she urged him on. She hated to wait. The tip of his tongue glided down her pussy, splitting her soft lips to taste her sweet juices in the center. His strong hands held onto her ass as she bucked wildly.

"Oooooh, just like that," she gasped as she watched his head move between her legs. She couldn't open her legs wide enough. She wanted him to taste her, lick her everywhere. Tenderly, she reached down and push his black hair out of his face. Her eyes connected with his for a second before they rolled into the back of her head as she moaned. He moved slowly to capture her clit. He began to suck and hum as he penetrated her with his two fingers. She wanted to cum so desperately, but not into his mouth.

"But it feels so good," she groaned, speaking to her inner self. It wasn't like before where it was rushed. This time he was slow, practiced. It felt as if he was drawing her into a trance as she pumped her hips in time with the movement of his fingers until she finally gave in. Her entire body stiffened. Her thighs trembled around him. He opened his mouth, covering her quaking hole to suck up every drop of her release.

Slowly, he licked his lips, then wiped them with the back of his hand. He got to his feet to stand before her. Calico's eyes widened at the size of the bulge stretching his pants. This was the first time they were able to see each other in the light. She had *felt* him, but never *seen* him. Rolling off the bed, she reached under her left arm, and unzipped her dress. The weight of it causing it to fall to the floor in a heap. She closed the space between them. He reached out his hand to draw her closer as he lowered his head to begin to suck on her large nipples.

"Wait," she ordered after a few seconds. She ignored his annoyed glare. If he thought she was stopping him because he had changed her mind, the man was a fool. There was only one thing that was going to be able to cool her fever. She grabbed his shirt, jerking it out of his pants. She stole a glimpse of him while her hands raced down the row of black buttons.

Andreas narrowed his eyes as he watched her push open his shirt. He told himself there was no rush. She was here. He had all night to explore and get lost in her sweet pussy. She smiled at him as it fell from his arms. Suddenly, he felt anger began to mix with his lust due to a thought that invaded his mind.

How many times had she done this since their time together? How many fucks in the backseat had she added to her list?

The hungry smile she had on her wet lips while she unbuckled his pants and opened his pants was starting to mock him. He bit the bottom of his lip in an attempt to gain control of his unreasonable temper. Shit, it wasn't as if he hadn't fucked his share in the two years since being with her. Like a robot, he reached over his head and removed his t-shirt.

Completely unaware of the cause for his intense expression, Calico marveled over his chiseled, tattooed body. He resembled more of a Greek god than an actual man. She had seen many ink jobs, but nothing as detailed as what he had painted onto his skin. It started high on his forearm with what looked like a 3D image of a Mayan temple that stretched up his shoulder. It then blended into a symbolic image that included an Egyptian pyramid, a clock, and ravens that covered the entire left peck on his chest. Deciding to investigate that later, her eyes zeroed in on the impressive dick that stood stiff, thick, long, and proud.

Andreas was shocked out of his thoughts at the feel of her hot breath on the mushroomed tip of his head.

Why risk the time over bullshit? Look at the way she's looking at your dick. Oh, Lord her lips are soft. Now, she's licking it. Anytime now. Anytime now, she going to open wide and-

"Fuck," he snarled. Her mouth instantly took him to another place and time. He was amazed at how much of his length disappeared into her mouth and down her throat. He pressed her downward until he felt her throat close around him. He closed his eyes as she began to gag and shower his cock with her saliva.

"You need to stop," he warned, hoarsely. He took a step back, but she held onto his ass to keep him in her mouth. "I can't wait, Coco," he admitted in a deep, husky voice. Not taking no for an answer, he pulled her to her feet. "This is where I need to be," he whispered. His strong hand parted her legs to cup her pussy. He stared at her in awe as she rode his open palm, leaving it wet.

Calico didn't care where he fucked her just as long as he got on with it. She was ready to explode. Without warning, she backed away from him, marched across the room to her purse, and brought it over. Quickly, she emptied the contents onto the bed. Snatching up a foil wrapper, she handed it to him.

"Put it on."

Andreas glanced behind her at the seven other packages that had landed on the mattress.

"Are you trying to tell me something?" he teased.

She rolled her eyes. "I'm telling you to slide that on," she panted.

He ripped it open with his teeth as he allowed her to guide him over to the bed. He stood at the side of the bed while she crawled on, awarding him with a clear view of her wet cunt glistening up at him. He felt his dick lunge forward as if it was going to detach from his body to bury itself inside if he continued to take too long. He joined her on the bed, at last. He blinked at the speed that she rolled off the bed, and pushed him back into a sitting position. Andreas bit his bottom lips and let out a moan as her hand gripped his long, thick dick.

Neither one realized they had been holding their breath until the loud exhale echoed throughout the room when he began to penetrate her body. His hand came up to rest on her hip as he guided her downward, filling her, stretching her with each blessed inch of his pulsating cock. He leaned forward and kissed her neck. He found himself focusing on the tempo of her rapid pulse.

"If I could live in you, I would," he confessed into her ear. "Shit, you're tight."

"I would think so. You were the last person in it."

She was so caught up in her own experience she didn't see how her words had affected him. There was pure shock reflected in his eyes. He had assumed that she would have been with others in that span of two years. However, the truth was that she felt the same way she did on that night in his backseat. Now he understood her fever pitch. He eyed the wrappers at the end of the bed with determination. He was going to mark her, fuck her, possess her. He began to describe in detail how her pussy felt around him. Like before, she responded to his words, as he knew she would. He knew just what to do to take her higher. He enjoyed watching her every expression, and hearing her every moan until he lost control. He leaned back with his weight resting on his left arm while he stared at her while she rose and fell upon his hard dick.

Calico paused to shift her weight to her feet instead of her knees before she began to leap on his cock like a frog. With each downward movement, the sounds of their bodies colliding vibrated off the walls. She felt him deeply. She enjoyed the pleasure and the slight pain of each stroke as he thrusted upward to meet her until she collapsed against him.

Swiftly, he rolled over, still inside her. He paused long enough to slide his arm under one of her thighs. He lifted her leg until it rested against his chest. He rotated his hips slowly as he leaned forward, penetrating and stretching her pussy even further. He was amazed that she was able to get even wetter in pleasure. He hated when his lovers became dry after a few strokes which took the fun out of the sex in his opinion. The thought of his dick being rubbed raw from dry friction never appealed to him. He found her open, natural excitement refreshing. It made him want to push her further. It made him want to see just how much she had to give him.

"I want you to turn my cherry out," she whimpered.

"Your words... I've warned you."

She smiled wickedly, "But I'm just speaking what's on my mind. I want you to dislocate your back. I want to feel you in my chest. I want you to pump me 'til—"

Andreas covered her mouth and began to kiss her deeply to stop the stream of lustful words that were wreaking havoc on his control. His hips kept in tune with his kiss. He gave her what she requested and a hell a lot more. He arched his back and searched for the right spot. He knew he had it by the way she began to shake. He could feel her walls began to clench and become slippery as he slid back and forth down her hot, tight passage.

"That's it... give it to me. Let me feel it jump," he grunted. He reached down and lifted her hips to make his contact even closer, even deeper, as he thrusted harder.

It felt like being hit by lightning. The nerves in her entire body were all lit up like a Christmas tree at one time, as her orgasm came like a tidal wave crashing against her. All she could do was hold on while it rocked her body until it was ready to bring her back to Earth. Andreas waited until she opened her eyes.

"Are you back with me?" he teased.

"Yes," she chuckled. "I think I'll need help walking, though. Oh, don't do that," she hissed.

"Don't do what?" he asked as he pretended not to know what she meant. His strokes were long when he began to move inside her again. He knew that right after her orgasm, he could make her come back to back if he drilled her slow and hard. In a matter of seconds, he watched as she threw back her head and screamed in ecstasy. He kept her in a steady routine of taking her to the clouds, then bringing her back down to Earth, only to start the cycle all over again. The bun on top of Calico's head had given way long ago from her sweating, thrashing, and being moved throughout the room as he had his way with her on the floor, against the walls, on the private deck, and on the chair.

"I think you have one more in you," he panted in her ear from his position behind her hours later, finally back on the bed. Andreas heard her moan of protest, but the way her cunt clenched when he rotated his hips said otherwise.

"Lay flat," he whispered. She had been up on her hands and knees for a while as he plowed into her. He waited for her to rest. He pressed his chest against her back for a second as he forced her right leg up with his knee. Coming up on his elbows, he began to move in her slowly. She buried her head into the pillow as he thrusted deeply, only for him to withdraw to his tip before he entered her again, forcing her to experience every glorious, thick inch of him. Moving his hand into position, he began to rub her clit.

"It won't be long, will it? I can feel you getting wet again. Soon you'll be raining down that brown sugar. Oh, that's it."

This time he didn't wait until she climbed down from the mountain top to take his release. He shoved her leg up high, rested his head on her shoulder, and picked up the pace until he pumped his hot cum into the rubber.

"Thank you, Lord," he moaned, unable to move a muscle. He waited for her to say something. When she didn't, he leaned forward to see she had already fallen asleep.

"Thank goodness," he mumbled. Having a determination was one thing, and having the strength to actually see it through was another. He'll go through the other rubbers starting in a few hours before he left for the office. Gripping the base of his cock, he withdrew from her unconscious body. A deep frown creased his brow. There was cum in the rubber, but he would have thought there would be a lot more than what was actually there. He squeezed the tip of the plastic and felt his heart leap in his chest. He didn't know how long he stared at the pearly drop on the tip of his finger. He hung his head.

I told you to switch rubbers. There were seven others right there. But OH NO, you didn't want to get out long enough to do it. You were fuckin her for over three hours, FOOL! the voice in his mind shouted. With a jerk, he tugged the rubber off, rolled out of bed, and flushed it down the toilet.

Chapter 4

Calico smiled. She had felt what he was doing a while ago, but she chose to continue to play sleep anyway. The feel of the mushroomed tip of his cock as he rubbed it against her leg, finally made her crack one of her gray eyes.

Andreas knew she had been pretending. After he was able to calm down enough last night, he decided to follow what his Grandma had taught him. He had meditated on her words, her voice, and before long, he had fallen asleep with Calico in his arms. Waking up next to her was both strange and exciting at the same time. It was an experience he could count on only one hand, and those times were all drug or liquor induced, never by choice.

"Finally," he said, happily, as he rolled on top of her. He positioned himself between her legs.

"Were you waiting long?"

"Long enough to start considering starting without you," he smiled, flashing her that devilish dimple.

"Mm, I can catch up really fast," she moaned, grabbing his ass. "What are you doing?"

He held up the washcloth for her to see before he began to wipe her cunt down. Tossing it to the floor, he replied, "It's said breakfast is the most important meal of the day," he winked as he started to move lower.

Calico looked at the patterns on the ceiling as she waited for the pleasure to begin.

**

Two hours later, they were both fed, showered, dressed, and extremely satisfied as they walked hand in hand down the dock to their waiting cars. He had the Ranger Rover brought over for her to use while she was posing as his girlfriend. It bothered him that after only a short time with him, he didn't know if that was all that he wanted it to be, just an act. Of course, that's the line he used to get her to this point, but now that he was into it, the thought had already come around what was next. When everyone had what they wanted, when the plan he was preparing was put into motion and was complete, Calico would return back to her life and what then?

Then that means you'll have to tell her the whole truth. Do you really think she's the type of girl that could handle that?

He stole a quick glimpse of her smiling face as she went on about something.

And what about you? You've been holding back, too. You tell her to be herself, while you've been working overtime to keep it all in.

Case in point, when he had received the voicemail while they dressed after their bath together. It had taken all his mental power not to let the rage shine through. He was sure the sound of his teeth chipping under the force of him grinding them could be heard. He knew his response was tight when he lied to her about it being a text about work. It didn't have a damn thing to do with work, but it had everything to do with that fat ass, big headed fucker, Russell.

"Aw, my hand," groaned Calico.

Andreas back away from her as if she had burned him. He ran his hand through his hair and took a calming breath.

"I promise everything will be alright," she ensured him. Coming up on the tips of her toes, she kissed him.

"I'm sorry. I was thinking about the shit I was getting ready to walk into," he mumbled, honestly. "I have something I want to tell you tonight."

Solemnly, she nodded her head. There was something off about him. Quickly, she got into the SUV. He told her that the address to the club was programmed into the GPS. She could ponder what was up with him later. Right now she had a job to do. For the last few days, she had been practicing the ways of some of her favorite mystery detectives. What they all had in common was that they pumped people for information by talking to them like they were friends. Sure she knew that this was real life, but putting on an act around people was something she was good at. All the countless number of hours at her office having to listen to the trifling issues and drama on the job, had prepared her well.

Andreas watched her turn into traffic on her way to the club. He would have loved to have gone there with her, but doing so would have exposed him a lot sooner than he was ready. He wasn't ready to ruin the fantasy just yet.

**

"What the hell is this?" grunted Calico forty-five minutes later when she parked the car in the virtually abandoned parking lot. She looked down at the cream-colored, spaghetti strapped jumper that fit tightly at her ankles, paired with matching heels she had chosen to wear. She was clearly overdressed for this place. She could have laughed at that thought, but she wasn't in the mood to do so. With a sigh, she removed her heels and traded them for the flats she had shoved into her purse.

Why would they want to redo a place like this? It's not like customers come here for the atmosphere, she wondered.

Questioning her location, she looked at the GPS mounted in the dashboard one more time to ensure that the address she had programmed in the system was actually the large building before her. Of course, she heard of the place. Everybody in Miami had heard of the infamous *King of Diamonds* strip club. From the music, to the celebrity sightings, to the flexible, tight as hell dancers, it was considered the NBA of tits and ass. She just never thought that she would be working there in any capacity. She had thought she was going to an upscale club with colorful lights, a bar, dance floor, maybe a place for live music given Russell's money.

Her legs felt like weights as Calico unwillingly walked up to the front door. It took her eyes a few seconds to adjust to the dark lighting in the main entryway. When they did focus, her outlook on the gentleman's club did a complete 360-degree turnaround. One by one, she took in what was considered the hall of fame that was displayed on the wall. In perfectly placed frames along the off white wall she saw famous singers like Beyoncé, Rihanna, Katy Perry, to rappers like Trina, TI, Drake, Lil Wayne, Jay-Z, to Floyd Mayweather scattered all over the area. Even Justin Bieber had managed to be seen there. She walked down the narrow hall and paused as she realized just how big the place was. Not only that, the place smelled from the water damage. With her designer's eye, she was able to see that the place hadn't been a hole in the wall. The lower level had been divided into distinctive sections. There was a main stage in the center of the floor with three stripper poles. Along the outskirts of the room were three smaller stages that were slightly elevated to give the room depth. The second level had café type table and chairs that overlooked the lower level. It also held a super exclusive VIP area. The entire place had been brightly colored to that point that she felt as if she was in a circus instead of a strip club.

"Who the hell are you?"

She had been so lost in her surroundings, she hadn't even noticed that the dark-skinned blonde had entered the room. She opened her mouth to speak up and then snapped it shut. It was obvious that the woman didn't like her from the nasty way she was glaring at her. She was used to insecure women trying to flex whenever she came around. She knew she had to set the tone from the starting gate.

"I'm Calico. I was hired to design the club after the damage." She made sure that when she spoke it was crisp and held a haughty air. She wanted to let the chick know that there was a difference between the two of them. Calico didn't care that the woman chose to shake her ass for dollar bills, but she wasn't going to be treated badly just because she didn't do it, too.

The girl tossed her hair over her shoulder and laughed. "I know your stiff ass wasn't trying to be no dancer," she finished with a nasty expression on her smooth face.

"You need to shut the fuck up and go clean out that damn locker like I told you," a deep male voice came from behind the bar. That was the only thing male about the tall man, Calico noticed as the tranny walked over to them. If it hadn't been for the booming voice, she would have thought that the medium breasted man was actually a woman. His short haircut was on point and very fashionable. She scanned his womanly shaped body and wondered if he was still packing or if he had gone all the way and had traded in his cock and balls for a purse.

"Don't mind that cunt, hon. She just mad that she was caught tricking on the side," he explained as he eyed Calico closely. He got the call last night that she was coming to get started, but now that she was standing in the middle of the club, she looked like a white rose in a field of weeds.

"You going to have to do something about that," he warned, finally speaking after such a long pause. From her questioning gaze he finished. "You too damn nice. I can see it like a bright beam radiating through those gray eyes of yours. Are those contacts, by the way? Never mind," he waved. "I'm LaFaye," he said instead as he held out his ringed hand for her to shake.

He smiled at the way she took his hand, firm, and he told her so, "Firm don't like limp things, you get me?" he winked. Without a word, he walked away forcing her to fall in step. He glanced over and laughed briefly at the sight of her digging into her Michael Kors bag to produce a pad and a camera. She followed him throughout the front main area. They discussed layout, concept, colors, and lighting. He was impressed that she actually knew what she was doing. She asked all the right questions.

"That's it," LaFaye announced an hour later, much to her happiness. "Did you record all of that?" he questioned, crossing his arms.

"I think so, yea. I can see why you run the place so well. Of course, nobody has to worry about you with the girls."

"I hope me being this way isn't going to be an issue?" he asked as he pinned her with a narrowed gaze.

"No."

"Good, cuz I wouldn't give a fuck if it did. Honestly, I get so much drama from these bitches that work here."

"Really? Why the would they be worrying about you?"

"Damn, well don't say it like that, shit," he grunted as he walked behind the bar to pour each of them a drink. "The competition, boo," he whispered. "My tits are better than theirs, and believe it not, a whole below is all the same in the dark. Hell, even better compared to these broken down cunts. You can look at me like that, but you'll see," he promised.

She had to admit, the smooth cappuccino colored skin man was gorgeous. He didn't look like a back alley or neighborhood drag queen that looked more like a man dressed up for Halloween. No, Lafaye had crafted his art. His makeup and hair was flawless. The hormones that he took had to be on the better end of the quality spectrum. He was definitely not a Bruce Jenner type that still held the masculinity of a man. The man that once was there had been completely replaced with a softer, more natural version of a RuPaul. She could see how a man would have had no problem blurring the lines to sleep with him.

"I thought the place was closed until the work is done?"

"Oh, yeah, officially it is, but we've been hosting private gatherings. The girls have to still pay their rent. Besides, the men and women that come don't mind. You can just work around them. So, how long before the grand opening?"

"Oh Lord," she sighed.

"Oh, don't say the Lord's name in a hell like this. What the fuck is wrong with you?" he spoke as he slapped her hand, completely forgetting his last question. "I know your brother, Rush," he said slowly.

Calico's thin eyebrow went up. "In what way?" She couldn't put nothing past Rush.

"Not like that, hon. Don't get me wrong, I would love to give the pipe to your brother, but I know he's straight. What I mean is he told me why you're here."

She wasn't going to assume that he knew the real reason she was there. "Oh," she responded with a straight face.

LaFaye paused and tilted his head while he searched her face. "He said that you were here on a seek and find mission. I've also been threatened by a very powerful man to keep an eye on you, which surprised the shit out of me. He didn't strike me as the one that got attached. It makes me wonder what else there is about you that no one is telling. All I'm saying is that there are more people working with you than you might think. However, I would be careful *who* you trust," he warned. He saw the confusion in her eyes.

She knew only one man that he could have been talking about. She had no clue why he referred to him as powerful. Andreas was rich, but not powerful. Then again, in a place like this where the number of bills you were willing to use to make it 'rain' spoke volumes, maybe they were talking about the same person after all. How many times had he been to the club for him to have such a close relationship with LaFaye? Enough times to feel comfortable strong-arming the man into doing his bidding? She wanted to ask LaFaye to tell her more. She only knew

Andreas within the confines of their agreement. She didn't really know him at all. However, she thought it was better to keep her mouth closed. The less she said about herself, the better chances of not being found out. Not to mention the fact that he could be testing her. She remembered his warning about her being too nice.

"So, are you saying you're someone that I can trust?"

"Oh, come on girl. I might not have all the plumbing, but I'm a bitch, and you know that a bitch can't be completely trusted."

"Then why you—"

He held his hand up to stop her. He had said all he was going to say. "Why does a woman do anything, if not for love?" he smirked before he shifted the conversation. "Now, like any place you got the field and the big house."

Calico swiveled on her chair to follow his gaze. She had seen the wall of mirror before they were on the second level. He hadn't shown her that place or the area where the dancers changed, yet.

"I know you can't tell it cause the lights are off, but that there is the place to be. A lot of high rollers and deals go on up there, but nobody just walks in there, understand?" he finished in a rush. They both heard the loud cackling that was coming from the back area where the girls were.

Calico rolled her eyes while she put her mask back on when she heard the same trifling chick from before speak her name to the other girls she had yet to meet. She had no qualms about fuckin' the whore up if it came to that. She had a new confidence when it came to throwing hands. After weeks of fighting and mixed martial arts she had taken at the Y to release some built up frustration due to the issues at work, she knew she could hold her own. It also helped to know that she had a neon colored Taser in her purse as well. By the time the group had gotten to her and LaFaye, she had calculated that she would have enough time to light the bitch up after she rammed her head on the side of the bar. She turned on the stool and positioned her weight to ensure that she would be able to move quickly if the girl got froggy and decided to jump.

"LaFaye, aren't you going to introduce us to the visitor?" asked the pretty Asian woman.

"I don't see the reason he should when all I heard was my name being tossed around," smirked Calico.

LaFaye wasn't fast enough in hiding the shocked expression on his face. One moment she had been the smart, soft spoken woman only to become the street talking chick that was letting every female know she wasn't the one to play with. He realized then that it should be him, that treaded lightly with Calico. She was much more than what she seemed. For the first time, he wondered if he was the one that was being played in this game.

"Hold up, this little bird has teeth, but there's no need to be a bitch, sweetheart. I don't give a damn as long as you don't get in the way of my money," explained the tanned china doll.

"Shit, you just kissing ass 'cause you heard she was Rush's sister and you been chasing that dick for the last month," the milk chocolate, small chested girl with the short bob and tattoos smiled, which made the diamond studs that were placed perfectly in her dimpled cheeks dazzle.

"Bitch, shut the fuck up," chuckled the short shapely Asian girl as she shoved her friend.

"Alright, girls," shouted LaFaye as he clapped his hands like a mother hen. "Calico, this is Rain and this one here is Brandy," he pointed first to the Asian girl than to her pierced friend. "The jealous hoe here is Chanel, and this here is Jasmine," he finished as he pointed to a pretty young girl that Calico wondered if she was even eighteen.

Chanel rolled her eyes. "Why the hell you sitting there sipping a rum and coke when you need to be working on getting this place opened?"

Calico snatched up her pad and handed it over to Chanel. "Tell you what, why don't you write down the things you would like me to do, so I can rip them up later because I don't give a damn about your opinion," replied Calico, crisply.

LaFaye started to walk from around the bar. He didn't need the girls getting into a fight. Andreas would kill him if Calico had to throw hands, although he was sure she would stomp Chanel's ass into the ground. The girl was nice, but there was also a lethal strength in her that said she wasn't selling wolf tickets. One thing he had learned from Jasmine was that it's the quiet ones when pushed that shocked the hell out of you. All his muscles were on high alert as he came to stand next to the women. Now that he thought about it, he would let Calico get a few punches off before he broke it up. He knew that that was mean of him, but the bitch needed a good ass kicking.

"How the hell you gonna talk about somebody when you should be working on your own act? That shit you been doing is so fuckin' played out. If you just gonna suck dick, then you need to get the hell out," grunted Brandy.

"Well, damn hoe. What the hell got into you?" questioned LaFaye. He was ready for a girl on girl, but he didn't know about having to break up a mob.

"Nothing, I just get tired of all that shade she always throwing every which way. I mean, we all have a pussy here, right? Well, you will after you save up for one," she directed at LaFaye with a wink.

"That's right, and the best thing is mine won't bleed," he countered.

"Well, maybe if your man is doing it right," added Calico which caused everyone to laugh and give her high fives for her quick wit.

"I like that. You gone fit in just right, hon," praised Rain as she eyed Calico closely. She had no doubt that the two of them were going to be thick as thieves. The girl had something about her. If a person was smart enough to recognize it, they would want to be in her corner if anything went down. Rain pulled up a chair next to her while the other girls walked over to the main stage to work on their acts for later tonight. LaFaye strolled over to give suggestions about the routines, leaving the two of them alone.

Calico watched the dancers in silence for a few minutes before she spoke. "I'm not going to get you in with my brother if that's what you hoping for." It wasn't as if she would have anyway. He had ruined her life enough. She didn't want to condemn the girl to a life of pain and disappointment.

"I don't need your help to get what I've been getting for the last three weeks, hon."

Rain smirked and wiggled her nose at Calico as she tilted her head to the side as if to say, *Ha, Bitch* with her reaction.

"Really," whispered Calico with a blinding smile. If it took her pretending she was happy, then that's what she had to do. She was here for information. The quicker she got it, the faster she could pass it along.

"You can't tell your business in a place like this. Many of them will sell you out to Russell if it means getting a little something from him."

"What he got to do with you and my brother?"

"That man wants what everyone else has. If he knew that Rush and I were messing around, he would all of a sudden be all interested and shit," explained Rain.

Calico couldn't help but notice the shiver that went through the pretty girl's body. She had to fight the same reaction from overtaking her. She had never liked her employer. Then again, most people very rarely liked the person, or company they worked for. It was always the 'Us' against 'The Man' mentality. However, she was beginning to recognize there was a much deeper reason to not like or trust Russell.

"I work for Russell at one of his *other* businesses. I had no idea he was involved in so much stuff. When I saw him he seemed nice and...." She let her words trail off because she didn't think whatever she had said would have sounded believable.

Rain tilted her head. "You must be blind, but to each his own. I know he can put on that act whenever he's around upstanding people, but there isn't something right about the man. If you've seen and heard the things I have when he's here... you'll see."

She wanted to press Rain for more details, then thought it was better she didn't know. Now that she looked at her, she wasn't too surprised that her brother went for the girl. Other than her full breasts and butt, she was real petite. She leaned over and studied the colorful ink that was on her left shoulder and arm. Rain had a sweet, soft way about her that Rush would find desirable. No doubt he played the girl like a fiddle.

"Well, you don't need to worry about me saying anything about you and Rush. What's up with that one?" questioned Calico as she gestured with her head toward Jasmine who was now on the stage, switching the conversation. She was quiet and shy off stage, but came alive when she was under the lights with the pole in her hand. She was even better than the other ladies that had been doing it longer than the young girl.

Rain leaned in and lowered her voice as if what she was about to say could be heard over the booming music.

"I don't know if you've met him, that's Chubby's baby girl," Rain paused long enough for Calico to digest her words. "Yeah, I know for a fact she isn't even eighteen yet, but Russell got her working here."

"Why the hell is she here? Why would Chubby have her doing this?"

Rain threw up her hands and straightened back up. "I don't know the whole story, other than if the big dog barks they all gonna fall in line. Like I just said, something ain't right."

Calico opened her mouth, but closed it when she noticed the people that were entering the dark club. LaFaye jumped up, turned off the sound system, and walked over to a man that she had never seen before.

"What's going on?" she asked Rain. It was clear to see that something was up. The whole mood was so tense, she could almost reach out and touch it. Soon she saw Rush walk in behind Russell and Wanda. She could tell that he had a fresh set of bruises on his face since the last time she had seen him four days ago. Bruises caused by Andreas's hands, but who added to them? Half of her was happy to see that he was still alive and kicking. But the other part of her, the part that was still pissed at his betrayal, made her turn away. The expression on everyone's face was too damn serious for this to be just a meet and greet with a few lap dances.

"I've been here with you, so how should I know," snapped Rain. Her large brown slanted eyes looked worried as they stared at Rush. She quickly broke her gaze before Russell could notice she had been looking at his do-boy. "Fuck," she mumbled before she addressed Calico's questioning gray eyes. "It must be big, whatever happened. Those men are the other five *Dons* that run Miami."

"What the hell is a *Don*?"

"Girl, stop acting stupid," demanded Rain in response to Calico's innocent question. Her gaze narrowed as she regarded her angry face. She wondered if the girl was putting on an act or if she really didn't know how things ran or even what her brother had been doing for the last two years.

"Okay, listen... the town is cut up into five pieces with each *Don* running things. You know drugs, guns, clubs, and females if they're into that stuff. Even if they aren't the ones actually doing it, they still get some of the kickbacks from the people they *allow* them to do it. This way, they all have each other backs like knights from the round table from Camelot, you know, but not everyone at the table likes to play nice... you get me?"

"What you two whispering about?"

Calico and Rain both jumped at the sound of Rush's voice behind them. They had been so focused on their conversation that they hadn't even notice him coming up. He had been secretly happy to find the two of them together. Now him talking to Rain wouldn't raise any eyebrows. Calico swirled around on the bar stool to greet her brother, only to stiffen when she realized he wasn't alone. She wasn't prepared to see Andreas standing there next to him. There was a strange expression on his handsome face that she couldn't name. Her eyes darted back and forth between him and Rush as she tried to figure out why Andreas was even there in the first place. She could understand her brother's presence, but why if what Rain had said was true, that this was an important meeting of the *Dons,* was he there? Her gray eyes caught sight of Wanda watching them closely from one of the tables she was standing near.

What the hell is going on? Calico wondered.

She swallowed hard as she tried to keep her composure, but she was afraid at the way they were looking at her as if they knew something that she felt she should and now wanted to know.

"Is everything alright?" pressed Rain, completely unaware of Calico's pounding heart that seemed as if it was in her throat, choking her.

She shifted in her chair, and smiled instead of speaking, out of fear that her voice might fail her.

"The shit hit the fan with another one," mumbled Rush while he pretended to be talking about the bottles on the shelves behind the bar.

"What...when...I didn't hear anything?"

"Early this morning, underneath an overpass. We made sure that the cops that responded were on the payroll, so hopefully we can just bury it like the others, but they're pissed. With camera phones, it's only a matter of time before the DEA or the news gets wind of this," replied Rush as he looked down at his sister even though he was answering Rain's question.

"What are you guys talking about?" hissed Calico.

"That new drug on the streets."

Rain had answered the question before she even knew what she had said. She saw Rush's face turn fierce instantly, as he played the part of a brother that was trying to keep his sister out of the secrets going on.

Andreas's eyes hadn't left Calico's face from the second he had entered the building. When he had gotten the call to attend the meeting at Russell's club, he had tried to arrange it to be changed to a different location, but it had been too late. There was nothing he could do but deal with the aftermath of his presence being there and all the questions that it would bring. He had no doubt that it had been intentional on Russell's part to have them all meet up here instead of somewhere else. The blinding smile the man had given him as he had passed him in the parking lot, said it all. There had never been any love between the two of them. The man had always done underhanded things to cause his family problems. When he didn't see him as a threat, Russell was able to hide his feeling toward him, but Andreas was never stupid. He always knew the man's true feelings concerning him.

"So, do you think you'll be able to work your designing magic?" he asked. He wanted to use the opportunity to chat her up.

She glanced up to stare into his blue gaze. "I think so. It's not as bad as I had thought," she smiled.

"I knew you would be the woman for the job," he winked. He caressed her cheek as he made room between her legs to stand. "I hope I'm the reason your nipples are getting hard," he whispered against her lips before he kissed her.

Calico laughed as she leaned back against the bar, giving him a better view.

"Don't tempt me, Coco," he smirked. "If you have your info, I can meet up with you later for lunch again."

She tilted her head as she narrowed her eyes. "Are you dismissing me?"

He wanted to pick her up and physically kick her out. Instead, he chuckled as he stroked her arm. He could tell that she had taken note of how the others in the room were gawking at them. Her eyes were no longer on his, but was scanning the room behind him. His heart was racing even if he appeared to be relaxed. This was not how he wanted her to find out.

She glanced out of the corner of her eye to see Rain's slack jawed expression. Calico knew that he was handsome, but that didn't explain the reason for Rain's reaction.

Are you jealous? How could she not want him? Look at him, damn it!

She let her gray eyes scan his body and experienced the electrifying feeling of lust shoot through her core to her cunt. He had that swag about him that was a mixture of class, sexiness, and a commanding nature that she found mind blowing. He seemed so out of place in the company of the men assembled in the club with their tailored suits, diamond watches, and gold pinky rings. Then again, he could make a potato sack look good on his tall, firm, muscular frame. The only jewelry he wore was the gold cross and chain he had told her his grandmother had given him the day of his confirmation into the Catholic faith. Unlike the other men assembled there, he knew who he was and what he was capable of doing. The wetness she felt between her legs was a strong reminder of what he could do and had done to her some many times the prior night that had her crying out in ecstasy under his sure hands and mouth. She took a deep breath and was engulfed by his cologne and male scent that was his alone. She looked nervously at Rain. She could see others were nodding in their direction. Sensing she was out of the loop, she reached behind her to retrieve her things from the bar.

"Andreas."

She turned back just in time to see his expression turn dark at the sound of his name. She opened her mouth to speak but the shock she experienced stole the words right out of her mouth.

"Get your shit and leave, now," he ordered in growl. Without a word, he turned to acknowledge the man that had called his name.

Rain tapped a stunned Calico on her arm. "Why were you holding out on me?"

"What, what are you talking about?" stammered Calico. She didn't know what had just happened.

"Why didn't you tell me you were with a *Don*?" Rain grinned at her as if she was a celebrity.

Calico was happy that the short girl had lowered her head while she slid off the bar stool. That way she wasn't able to see her flabbergasted expression. She worked her mouth as she looked toward Rush to deny it. However, he confirmed it with a silent, *yes.* By the time

Rain glanced back at her, she had hidden her surprise under a smile. She prided herself for not giving into the rage she felt at that moment. How fuckin' stupid could she be? The money, the car, the warehouse, the gotdamn boat! It all made sense. How Rush went from working for him to working for Russell. When he had said that he and Russell were business partners, she had assumed a legal business. Well, assuming had just made an ass out of her. He was no fuckin' better than—

"Rain, that's enough," grunted Rush, finding his voice at last, and cutting into her mental rant.

"No, keep on going," Calico encouraged her with a blinding smile. She could feel her body began to shake from the rage she could barely contain. "I might be with a *Don*, but you seem to know a lot more than me," she chuckled. She could see the hesitation in the woman. She knew that Rain didn't want to do anything that would put her at odds with Rush, but Calico was going to make the chick spill the tea if she wanted to or not. "I'm listening," she pressed.

"Yeah, right...so..." she stumbled. "Your man is number two in the pecking order. His great-uncle over there...the one in all black is the number one man, so that gives Andreas a lot of power even if he is the youngest of all the *Dons*," Rain finished in pure awe. "I got to know your secret. I'm not going to lie, all the girls up in here, me included had been trying to get with him, but I can tell he's really digging you. The way he came up in here and showed everyone that you were his. That's some romantic shit."

Now she knew that it was Andreas that LaFaye had been talking about.

Calico's eyes sought out the man that Rain had mentioned to be Andrea's uncle. It was clear that he was the man that sat at the top from the power he seemed to exude. His power wasn't loud or brass, but he spoke in soft, almost hushed tones with slow movements. He was like an Al Pacino with blue eyes that seemed to be able to bore into a person's soul. She watched on in disbelief while he and Andreas spoke privately at one of the tables, as the other men stood at a discrete distance. Her breath caught in her throat and she had to gulp it down when Andrea's eyes moved to lock with hers. His eyes were unreadable as if he had closed off himself from her completely, but hers were open to him. He could see that his secret had been exposed. She knew what he was, and he could see the anger, betrayal, and confusion in her gaze.

Calico's eyes bore into the side of Rush's head, but he refused to look at her. Instead, he continued to concentrate on a spot behind the bar. The fact that he chose to not look at her spoke volumes. He knew. He had always known that Andreas was more than a businessman. He had known from day one, and he had purposefully placed her in the handsome Italian's path.

**

He had heard Rain whispering to Calico. He didn't have to be a fly on the wall to know what was going to happen next. As he had walked toward the waiting man, his gaze fell upon a smirking Russell. He sat down and attempted hard to follow what the man to his left was saying, but his eyes were trained on Calico and Rain. She had responded to the woman. She stood still with a blank expression as she listened silently. Calico then tilted her head as if she had misunderstood what had been said. A slow smile formed across her lips. Her head turned slowly in his direction. He had seen that smile before. To others, it appeared normal, and cheerful, but in the depths of her gray, glaring eyes had been something very different. Andreas knew that there was no telling how the chips may lay after today regarding him and Calico. Just like a changing wind, his worry was exchanged for the temper he was known for. He formed a tight fist and slammed it down on the table which caused the older man to jump in surprise.

"Are you alright?" questioned the man. His eyes went over to the woman that seemed to have Andreas's attention.

He ran his hand through his dark hair, pushing it back from his eyes, and took a deep calming breath and exhaled it loudly. The smile he flashed the man was a mixture of wicked and dangerous. It made Aldo sit back as a shudder ran down his spin.

"I've never know you to have a problem with a woman," commented Aldo, slowly. His Italian accent was still heavy after so many years in the States.

The sound of Andreas's chuckle only served to make the man feel even more uneasy. "You have no fucking idea."

The man regarded the chocolate girl closely as he pondered if she was the one that he heard about some time ago. If so, then he knew the reason for the boy's anger, even if he didn't know it yet. It only took one time, with the right person to change a man's life.

**

"Well, the club is closed for now. I'll show you the other areas later," offered LaFaye.

Calico nodded. At that second, all she wanted to do was leave.

"Why you making her go?"

Calico felt her heart stop. She wasn't ready, as she fought to get back into character. She couldn't afford to let anyone see that she was upset. There was nothing she could do about Rush and Andreas. She was here and she had a job to do, she reminded herself.

Chapter 5

"I thought she needed to go home for the meeting, sir," stumbled LaFaye under the hard glare of Russell's brown commanding eyes.

"What the fuck for? I'm paying her to do a job that had to be done, like yesterday. I'm losing too much money as it is. Shit, she screwing around with Dre. She's family," laughed Russell.

He had seen her and Andreas when he had walked into the building. He had been trying to make his way over sooner, but he had wanted to listen to the conversation his power grabbing wife was having with some of the other *Dons.* He would have killed the bitch long ago if he didn't need her to maintain control of the position he had gotten after her father had died. He had licked that man's boots for too many damn years until he had made enough contacts to ensure that after he killed the man, he would take over. He had no intentions of losing it all now because of her plotting ass. That's why the deals he had been making as of late were so important. Of course, the others weren't happy, but they could all kiss his ass. He was building an empire. One that wouldn't involve Wanda and would have him running all of Miami, not just a small territory.

"Are you sure I should be allowed in the room when you're talking business?" she offered. She knew that her being there was for the purpose of info gathering, but Rush could be the snitch. They didn't need two at the meeting. Besides, she just wanted to be alone with her thoughts.

Russell put his hand around her waist and pulled her to his side. "Don't let us keep you from working. Oh, and when you get done here, I need you to come by the office. There are some accounts you were working on that need to be explained."

"The only thing that needs to be explained is why you think I would *allow* you to touch her," remarked Andreas in a gruff voice. As soon as he had seen that greasy asshole step too close to her, he had gotten up on his feet. He didn't need his uncle tapping him on the leg to warn him. He had been watching on the edge of his seat the entire time. He didn't give a damn that this was Russell's club, in Russell's territory. He would kick his ass in his own home.

He turned and came face to face with the Italian towering over him. It was obvious that his ploy had worked. It made him feel good to know that toying with something that the man wanted, got under his skin. Just like he wanted the power, and position the young motherfucker had been given. Instead of him being bumped up in the ranks, Andreas had been given the second biggest piece of the Miami pie, and for what? Because of the old, dead hag's wishes? Because his old fashion uncle thought he was running the show? There had been so many times he had dreamt of shooting the man between the eyes when he started talking about honor, and the code, and how things had always been done. It was time for a new code, and who gave a damn about honor? This was a fucking war. It was the one that was willing to take what he wanted and hold it with an iron fist that should be in control. The old man had watched too many *Godfather* marathons.

Well, this is just the beginning of me taking what you want and making it mine, he thought with a smirk.

"I'm not concerned about her loyalty, but if you are then I suggest you stop messing around with her," challenged Russell.

"I think you're starting to believe your own hype, old man, if you think you can tell me where I can stick my cock. I'll stick it down your throat if you don't step the hell back," grunted Andreas as he took a step forward. He didn't give a damn at that moment. He was almost willing the man to react so he could smash his face in.

Calico didn't give a damn either. She was getting the hell out of there. Her eyes darted around the room. She could see that the other men in the room were looking forward to a showdown. No longer was Andreas the man she had laughed at and teased. She had picked up that change in him yesterday. That, mixed in with that confidence and increased sexiness, there was another element she couldn't name until now—danger. It both excited and frightened her to see the darkness within him. He was willing to fight for her. Just like the arrangement, he was willing to cover her by giving her his obvious power and influence to protect her. In spite of Russell's girth, she had no doubt that Andreas would come out the winner.

Rain had stayed in her spot by the bar to watch the fireworks, but now she had seen enough. LaFaye glanced back over his shoulder and mouthed to her to, *get the hell out of there.* Not stopping to look behind her, she pushed her way through the crush of bodies that were closing in around the bar. She could hear someone telling the two men to calm down before she ran through the front door into the parking lot.

Andreas glared at LaFaye while he grasped Calico's hand to give it a tight squeeze. He narrowed his eyes as he pinned her with his gaze. He didn't want her there, but he couldn't let her leave either. To do so would be sending a message to the others that he didn't trust her, which might cause a problem for her later. These men were powerful people that kept their true business dealing secret from the masses. They sat on church boards, sponsored kids' athletics, donated to charities, all to keep a good standing in the public eye. He saw her gulp hard before he handed her over to LaFaye to go stand behind the bar.

"We all know it's more than just big dog Russ trying to tell me who I can and can't be with. The damn man is drunk with power. He doesn't give a damn about the rules because he thinks he can just rewrite them, and we all are just going to bend over and take it in the ass," explained Andreas angrily.

Sensing they weren't going to make it to the private meeting room, Wanda took a seat with the others following suit. Russell bit his tongue over the fact that people still watched and followed her lead. He jerked out a chair and sat down slowly.

"He does have a point, Russell. You have caused us all a lot of trouble and this shit is getting out of hand," said an old Cuban, who was also a *Don*.

Russell regarded the sixty plus people in the room that was made up of the four leaders and their close advisers, lieutenants and assistants.

"You run things how you want, and I do things my way," replied Russell, annoyed.

"But the issue here is that your crap is crossing over into their backyard," snapped Wanda. He glared at her with his narrowed gaze.

"We weren't happy with you when this new drug hit the street, and we told you so. We asked you to stop pushing it, but you shrugged us off and did what you wanted. Now, this new stuff is making waves," added Aldo, Andreas's uncle, in a deep even voice.

"Waves... the stuff is turning people into face eating zombies. It's like the *Walking Dead* out there," barked Andreas.

"Plus, we ain't gonna be able to hide what's been going on which means Washington and the DEA," added the tall, dark-skinned Haitian with a head full of neat braids.

"We want to know where the drug is coming from. Who you got bringing it in?" questioned Aldo.

"You all are crazy if you think I'm giving up my contact so you can sell me out. You don't give a damn about the accidents, you just pissed cuz I'm getting it all," answered Russell as he got to his feet.

"Look, this is a partnership that was formed on an understanding that's served us all well for years. We didn't have no issues with Wanda's father when he was alive." Aldo had chosen his words to ensure it hit home and make the most damage. He was very aware of Russell's feeling about his wife and her father. He would have loved to know who on the panel had voted for the fool to get the position in the first place. That was one mystery that had yet to rise to the surface.

"Then the old man shouldn't have gotten his head blown off with a shotgun. I don't give a damn about his ass or how things were done. I'm fucking this cat now, and you all are in *my* house. I don't *need* you all cuz I can run my shit just fine without any of you. I don't need to explain my decisions to anyone. So, if you all want to stay to buy a drink, fine, but the club is closed," stated Russell firmly, dismissing them all.

Aldo placed his hand on Andreas's knee under the table to stop him from moving, and giving the signal to kill the power drunk man. He would have loved to have let him do it. Shit, he would have been willing to dirty his hands and pull the trigger himself, but it wasn't time yet. Patience was what he was telling his great nephew. They had too much to lose.

Calico remained still next to LaFaye behind the bar. Her mind had already leapt ahead of where to hide should someone decide to pull a gun in an attempt to kill Russell right then and there. She watched as he stared into the faces of his enemies. Smoothly, Wanda got to her feet, grabbed her purse and walked over to the bar. It was like the woman broke the spell that had fallen over the room. Soon, the frozen men began to thaw and move as they talked to one another and made their way outside.

She didn't know whether to fear or label Russell insane as she eyed him across the room talking to Chubby. Like the old OG that he was, he was dressed to the nines in his tailor made pinstriped gray suit with shiny black shoes. She wished she was closer to hear what he and Chubby were talking about because whatever it was, was important. She could tell by the way that the tall rat-faced man was leaning in to press his point that the conversation was a heated one. Finally, Russell responded in an annoyed fashion that sent a tight lipped Chubby walking away, still fuming to himself.

"I'm sorry you had to witness all of that. I'm even more sorry that you had to find out the truth about Andreas's occupation this way. That's why Russ forced the meet to be here. I really hope you don't give my husband what he wants by letting this come between you and Dre," pleaded Wanda. She frowned at the way Calico was holding her glass in her shaking hand.

"Calm down, calm down," mumbled Wanda. "I don't want you breaking shit," she stated as she walked behind the bar. "Give me that," she ordered as she took the glass from Calico's hand. Wanda gestured with her head for LaFaye to go away while she spoke to her. "I have *never* seen him act like that over anyone other than his Grandma," whispered Wanda, giving her a toothy grin.

"Is that supposed to make me feel special?"

"If you knew how crazy he was over that damn woman, yeah, it should. It was just the two of them. Then when she died late last year…" she shook her head. "If you think that he was a mess just then, you better be glad you didn't see him in rare form when his temper is in full affect. Look, all I'm saying is, for him to go off like that, there is a lot more going on between the two of you than just a little bump and grind. Now," she took a deep breath as she sat the glass on the shelf, "tell me how you're gonna make this hole in the wall great again."

Russell watched the number of people in the room began to thin out while he tapped his pinky ring. After what just happened, he had made an executive decision to reach out to order his people to double production in the lab. If they thought they were pissed now, what would soon be coming down the pipeline in a few weeks was going to shut them all down. This was going to be the deal to trump all other deals. His joy was short lived when he turned to see Calico standing behind the bar in deep conversation with his wife. He cursed under his breath. He just couldn't wait to choke the life out of Wanda. Everything that should be his, she always seemed to taint with her presence. His position and now that girl.

"The fuckin dike," he mumbled. At first, it had been a game that he enjoyed. Shit, what man wouldn't jump at the opportunity to screw another woman after fucking the same holes for so long. He used to enjoy the rush of sitting in a club with Wanda as she pointed out the different girls that they could take home for the night. The act of watching her walk over, talk to the girl, and convince the girl to go along was all part of the foreplay which made it even sweeter as he screwed the wet, tight, young cunt while the girl licked Wanda's pussy, before Wanda would get the girl off while the chick sucked his dick. It didn't take him long to realize that she was even better at making the girls cum than he was. Over time, they both began to seek their pleasure elsewhere to the point that they lived together, but didn't sleep together.

He began to walk over to the bar where Andreas was standing, while both he and Wanda listened to something Calico was saying. He was sure it was about the building. He had always found the girl desirable. However, now he found her irresistible. He widened his strides when he saw the two ladies come from around the bar to stand next to Andreas. The Italian took Calico's hand in his, but he could have sworn she had tried to pull away for a split second before she gave in to him. He gave her a toothy grin as she turned to acknowledge his presence.

"About those files..." Calico started slowly.

"Oh baby, you won't have time to worry about that, not with the work here, and keeping up with my demands," Andreas explained in a deep sensual voice. Not saying another word, he walked off, taking her with him.

"Don't forget what I said. I'll call you later," promised Wanda before Calico got out of earshot. She shared a glance with Russell before she smirked, then strolled away, leaving him in the club.

**

Calico offered him the respect of pretending to be cheerful until they reached the parking lot. In the hot early afternoon sun, she snatched her hand away. Frantically, she began to search her purse for the keys to the Rover. She knew they were in there, somewhere, but she was too angry at the moment to focus long enough to find them in the black gaping hole of her purse. Frustrated, she scanned the parking lot.

"Give me your keys," she ordered with her hands out.

Andreas eyed her as if she had fallen and bumped her head. "Excuse me."

"Give me your fuckin' keys," she spat, slowly. When he just stood there regarding her with a mixture of disbelief and humor, it elevated her anger to a new height. No longer willing to spare him the embarrassment in front of the few men still outside, she leaned forward quickly, snatching the keys out of his dumbfounded hands. She turned so fast he thought he saw the movement from her feet toss dust up into the air as she began to speed walk toward his Aston Martin.

"Calico," he called out before he broke out into a jog to catch up. He glared at Milky, the tall thin Haitian, and the others that were glued to what was going down in the parking lot with obvious amusement.

"Hurry up! Faster, Andreas!" Milky shouted, teasingly.

Andreas held up his middle finger which caused a roar of laughter to break out. His wide strides had him reaching the car a heartbeat after she did.

"I don't think you should be driving."

Silence.

"Can you even drive a stick? The gear shift is on the wheel not the…" his words trailed off at the murderous look she shot him from across the hood of car. "Calico, see, you're so worked up, you can't even open the door. I don't want you driving," he pointed out. He was doing his damnedest to not let his temper get the best of him.

"If I crash the damn car, you can just buy another one. You are a freakin *Don*, right?" she growled, pushing the lock release button. She groaned when she saw him open the passenger side door. She had been trying to figure out how to open just the driver side.

"Where are we going?"

"Look, you need to be quiet… *please,*" she barked. The car roared to life.

"Your seatbelt," said Andreas. His blue eyes sparkled as he bit his bottom lip. He had figured she could be a handful when she was mad, but he had never imagined this. Calico was so used to hiding her true feelings the majority of the time, that when she got to her limit, it was like a flood gate opening. He knew all he had to do was hold on and surf the wave until it was over. He watched her squeeze the wheel before she practically ripped the seat belt strap from the holder and clicked it, forcefully into place. He wanted to laugh, but he knew that doing so would only serve to make matters worse.

Aldo pushed the red square on his phone to stop the video recorder as the girl tore out of the parking lot. He tapped the driver to signal for him to drive away. He shook his head while he waited for the other person on the line to pick up.

"I have to talk to you," he stated.

"That bad, huh," the person responded.

"It went as expected," he shrugged.

"And Andreas?"

"After what happened today, he will do what he threatened he was going to do to end it," he smiled.

"Shit, whatever happened couldn't have been *too* bad. I can hear that goofy grin of yours a mile away."

"Oh, for Andreas, it's bad," laughed Aldo.

Chapter 6

He glanced down at his phone to check the time. She had been driving for the last forty minutes without a word. He had been trying to draw her out of her head with no success. As far as he was concerned, not knowing what she was thinking was the worst possible thing. t It meant that she didn't trust him which meant she would treat him the same way she handled everyone else in her life. Her walking around smiling, agreeing, nodding, telling them what she knew what they wanted to hear while she kept her true self bottled up inside. He rolled his eyes. They had been trying for the last three lights to make a right hand turn, but due to the afternoon Miami traffic, they had barely moved at all. He frowned at the sound of his stomach's constant protest to be fed. He hadn't eaten at a *Burger King* in years, but the one across the street was starting to look real tempting.

"I know. I know buddy," he whispered as he stroked his stomach. He made a show of clearing his throat and swallowing hard as if he was thirsty.

"I'm not going over there," she snapped.

"Well can we go somewhere? I'm about to pass out."

"I would if we weren't stuck in this damn traffic!" she screamed. "Why aren't these people working?"

"Can I make a suggestion of a place that's about thirty minutes away?"

"I don't care," she sighed.

He quickly plugged the address into the car's GPS. Next, he sent a text through to his phone, to make sure that by the time they arrived, they wouldn't have to wait to eat. It didn't take her long to see after breaking free from the deadlock, that they weren't going to a restaurant. The downtown, congested streets gave way to the residential landscape. She didn't put up a fight. She obeyed the navigation system's commands mindlessly as she was led deeper into an area that she would have never dreamt of straying into while driving her small 2011, black Scion hatchback.

"In 0.3 miles, turn right. Your destination, 3551 Main Highway will be on your right."

Calico slowed in front of a towering black ironed gate. A deep frown creased her brow. There was nothing there but trees. A house couldn't be seen as she leaned forward to peer into the overgrown foliage that a paved blacktop ran in the middle of to disappear into the shadowy abyss.

"Coco, you need to turn off the road, or someone's going to crash into the back of us," he warned, looking through the car door's side mirror to check the traffic behind them. He pulled out his phone and typed in a code.

Her eyes widen as the gate, magically began to open. Putting the car in motion, she drove down the long, shadowed, twisting driveway that seemed to go on forever.

"How big is your estate?" It was the first thing she had said actually to him in the last twenty minutes.

"It's 6.9 acres."

She halted the car when the massive house came into view. She was speechless at the sight of the Italian inspired home. Andreas shut the car off before he followed her outside. He stayed a few steps behind her to give her time to process what she was viewing. The house wasn't as tall as much as it was wide. She paused to glance at the angel statue that was nestled in the middle of the grass, which created a cobble stone roundabout drive in front of the mission styled entryway. Andreas waved the man away that had opened the door to greet them. Silently, she walked into the home. She was completely taken aback by the stucco walls, curved archways, exposed beam work in the ceilings, large windows, the brick stairs that lead to the upper floor, and the mixture of the chestnut wood flooring with the polished light tan tile. Even the choice of artwork, light fixtures, rugs, and furniture all worked together to make a person forget they were in an American and not in a home in the heart of old country in Italy.

"It's...wow," was all she could muster to say at first. "How big is it...the house?"

He smiled, wickedly. He knew what she had meant. "It's over 16,000 square feet with 6 bedrooms and 9 baths. There's a guest house, a pool, a water canal for smaller boats that will take you out to the ocean, and a huge yard in the back, too," he finished as he guided her through a set of double doors.

Calico examined the room to see that it was study, or sitting room of some kind that opened to the back yard. She followed her nose to find that food had been set up on a far side table for them. She stiffened at the sound of him closing the doors behind her.

Andreas silently locked the door for good measure to ensure there would be no escape for her. Of course, she could run into the backyard, but he knew she wouldn't get too far before he caught her. Taking a deep breath, he turned to face her. She hadn't disappointed him. She was standing with her feet apart, ready to do battle. He mentally cautioned himself to keep his temper in check. That she had a right to be angry- to a point. It was that point that was going to be an issue.

"Was all of this," she gestured with a wave of her hand. "what you wanted to talk to me about."

He could have lied, but now that the cat was out of the bag, he wanted to keep it that way.

"No."

She nodded her head angrily. "Hmm, so, what were you going to say?"

"I wanted to tell you about the plan I had to get the information without putting you at risk."

"Good! I'd like to hear it. Then, again no I don't. You just do what you do best so I can leave you the fuck alone."

He narrowed his eyes as he pinned her with his blue gaze. "You won't be leaving," he stated in a calm voice.

"Oh," she laughed. "This was just an *arrangement*," she reminded him. "With benefits," she added. "I will be leaving when it's all said and done," she promised him.

"You can't do that," he barked.

"Why not?"

"Because last night. there was a problem," he started. He took a deep breath and counted, mentally to 10.

"I'm listening," she pressed.

He bit down on his teeth. He wanted to slap that haughty look off her face. She could be a bitch, and he had been worried if she could hold her own in a life such as his.

He ran his hand through his hair. "Last night, when I pulled out, I noticed a problem with the rubber."

Calico stumbled back as I she had been slapped across the face. She had been mad, pissed, annoyed before, but know she was livid.

"I don't believe you," she grunted.

"Are you on the pill?"

Her silence was her only answer.

"In two weeks or less, we'll know. When it comes on, 'cause it will, I'm gone." She sounded more like she was trying to convince herself than speaking to him. "FUCK!" she screamed at the top of her lungs.

He had wanted to ask her if it was really all that bad to have his baby, but thought it was better to keep quiet. He had thought she had lost her mind when she started to laugh, but then he glimpsed the twisted look in her gray eyes.

"All this time that agent had me trying to catch Russell, when I'm fucking around with you. Shit, I'm sure if I just fucked him, I could get the info quicker. Sucking one *Don's* dick is no different than another's," she spat.

"What your mouth," he replied, coldly.

"I'm sure that's why Rush got me that job at the office. He was just pimping me out to yet, another *Don* after you hooked him up at the game," she went on.

"Calico please, I'm trying here," he hissed.

"I wouldn't even be here if it wasn't for you."

"Shut up," he thundered.

"You're no fuckin better than my punk ass brother," she shouted. Her shout turned into a scream a second later.

Andreas didn't let anything stand in his way. He closed the gap between them in a few large steps as he walked toward her, tossing the furniture out of his way to clear his path. Swiftly, he grabbed her arm and began to shake her like a rag doll. She felt her teeth rattling in her mouth at the force of his attack. Stopping abruptly, he narrowed his sparkling blue eyes while he took a deep breath as he fought to regain his rage. He shoved her away with a look of disgust on his handsome face.

"Don't you ever, EVER compare me to that fat motherfucker or your no good ass brother," he roared as he pointed his finger into her chest. "Dear God, I've never wanted to punch a woman until now, but let's talk about your brother."

Calico took a step back to give him room. She was scared that he might lose control of the very thin reign he had on his temper. She was finding out now that he talked with his hands when he was enraged.

"He didn't want to work. He didn't want to start at the bottom. I tried to keep him out of the business. I told him, but it only took him one time seeing Russell, and he was hell bent on working for the man. All he saw was the quick money. And what did he do with that money? He damn sure didn't share it with you," he held up his hand for her to be quiet. "No, instead he was going around town flossing and flexing like he's some big dog. And there you were, calling two, three times a day looking for him because you need his half of the bills. Oh, yeah I know all about that." He nodded when her expression turned confused. He walked away and took a seat on the couch.

"I tracked him down to tell him to take his ass home, or at least call you. Let me tell you what he said. He said he didn't give a damn about your ass. He said that you could use all that *cash* you had to pay the damn bills. The asshole was upset that you didn't give him any of that money that I had given you. Of course, I didn't tell him that. Instead I baited his ass. I said, hey...she might be saving that money for a new car or a business. He laughed. He said that you always thought you were better than everybody. I so wanted to smash his head in," he growled.

"I don't believe you. Rush has been paying his bil—"

"No," he fumed. "*I* have been *paying* his share. *Me*, not *him*! After I left him that day at the apartment of the chick he was shacked up with. *I* called the leasing company and paid his half of your rent. *I* came by your place and shoved that envelope into your mailbox that had three hundred dollars in it for your expenses. When I had heard about those break ins in your neighborhood, *I* was the one that arranged for you to move into the place you're living in now."

Calico was completely numb. There was no doubting what he was saying was true. He knew way too much for it to be a lie. She felt like her feet were heavy as she shuffled across the room to gaze down upon him. He was now leaning over with his head lowered to stare at the floor. She wanted to push his hair back from his face to see his expression, but the black locks obstructed her view.

"Then why did he tell the agent that I had taken money from him. I didn't have to..." her words trialed off.

"He played you. He had to do something to make you help keep him out of prison. That's why I beat his ass," he explained.

"Why did you do all that for me?" she questioned, softly.

"How the hell should I know?" he growled. "That's the same damn question she had asked me," he mumbled with a wave of his hand.

Calico turned her head to look in the direction he had gestured. Her eyes took in the antique desk positioned next to one of the large windows overlooking the backyard. She didn't have to ask who *she* was. She could almost see a woman sitting there working at the desk while Andreas ran around the backyard, or colored, or napped in the room with her. She reached up and pulled the tie out of her head. Her thick hair came cascading down her neck and shoulders. It's what she did at the end of a trying day to unwind. Tossing the decorative pillow out of the way, she plopped down next to him on the couch.

"So your grandfather was a *Don* and he left it to you?" she asked in her natural tone. She was hoping that he wasn't still upset."

"Yes and no," he sighed, straightening up in the chair before he slouched down with the back of his head tossed back. "When he died, my grandmother wrestled to keep control. She did what needed to be done to maintain the power. After she left she, she willed it all to me."

"And then it was your turn to do the wrestling," she added with a raised eyebrow.

"That's right," he smirked.

"I can see that you've become very good at it," she praised.

"Thank you," he smiled sneaking a glimpse of her.

"So is that her?" she asked.

He looked at her strangely, then glanced at the large vase that sat on the mantel of the fireplace. A deep frown creased his forehead. "No, that's just a vase."

"Oh," she chuckled, embarrassed. "So, long how she been gone. I mean, when did she die?"

"I really don't know," he answered sadly. "One day I came home and she had left. Then she sent me a letter with this flower she wanted me to plant in the garden for her. She said that she couldn't stand watching me play bedside nurse while she lay there dying. A few months later, my uncle Aldo called me to say that someone had told him that she had passed away, peacefully," he swallowed.

Calico wanted to hold him, but she knew it would have done nothing to take away the pain that shined so brightly in his eyes. She understood that the woman had meant well, but her actions had made his loss even harder for him to process. She had robbed him of his right to grieve. She had taken away his right to that last conversation. That last touch. That last, I love you. That last goodbye.

Touching his shoulder, "I'm sorry for *my* part of this argument. When I get started, because I hold so much, I tend to cut deep."

"I don't want you to hold anything back, but you were off the scale. You don't understand how your words can affect me. I don't know why, but they do. You gotta dial it back, Coco," he sighed.

She studied him as he continued to explain his point by reenacting her attitude with the facial expressions and her voice. After a while, she felt as if she was sitting at one of the school decks in a *Charlie Brown* cartoon. His mouth was moving, but all she could see was just how nicely shaped his mouth was. The way his bottom lip was slightly larger, and plumper than the top. Her eyes dilated as they scanned his face and chiseled jaw line. He hadn't shaved before they had left that morning, so his facial hair was darker than before. Her heated gaze continued downward over his muscular his chest. She pressed her lips together, and shifted her weight on the couch to enjoy the low throbbing that was building in her center. Her breath caught in her throat when her eyes saw that hem of his shirt had risen above his blue jean waist. It was up just enough for her greedy pupils to see the dark line of hair that ran down the center of his tight abs to disappear into his pants.

Blinking herself out of the sexual induced trance, she was amazed at the fact that he was still going in hard on her. She laid her head on his shoulder briefly. Then she rose her head. Calico opened her mouth and began to suck on his earlobe.

Finally, she thought, mentally. Her hand went to that spot she had spied earlier. She dragged his shirt up higher. Her hand seemed to have a mind of its own as it danced over his ripped abs.

"Take me to your room," she whispered in his ear.

That's all Andreas needed to hear. He gladly got to his feet, took her out stretched hand, and led her through the house, up the stairs, down the hall to the last door on the left. He opened the door to a room that wasn't the master suite, but it was big enough to be one. Curious to be in his space, she dropped his hand to walk deeper into the room. Her eyes took in everything in the masculine space from the multi-colored stained hardwood flooring, to the bright white walls, to the distressed wood furniture, to the large bed, and finally the huge TV that dominated an entire wall.

"Are there extra linens in here?" she inquired. She opened the large trunk that sat at the foot of his bed.

"Um, yeah and—"

"Other stuff," she chuckled. Her moving the covers and sheets around had produced his porn stash. "What's all this? Tapes, magazines...hold up, *Black Tails!*" she laughed, waving the magazine in the air. "And the pages are worn, too. Well, no one can say that you discriminate," she mumbled. She opened it and began to flip through the pages.

"What can I say? I like the female form," he smiled, strolling towards her.

Calico's eyebrow went up as she glared at him from over the magazine.

"One form in particular," he amended.

"Well, it does help that it's the *only* form you have here," she smirked, tossing the book back into the trunk.

"See," he said, frustrated "Here I am trying to set the mood and you're messing it all up."

She stuck out her lower lip in a cute pout. "If that's what you were going for, all you had to do was this." She reached out, grabbed his hand, and placed it so it cupped her pussy. "Or I can do this?" She continued as she unzipped his pants and reached inside to pull out his cock. "Or this?" She whispered as she bent down, opened her mouth, taking his mushroomed head inside.

Andreas gathered her hair into his fist while he watched his hard dick play peek-a-boo. He closed his eyes and concentrated on the pleasure her mouth was creating and the slurping noises that echoed throughout the room. Behind hooded lids, he gazed down upon her head as she made love to him with her mouth. He twirled the straps that tied at her back to hold the jumpsuit together. He tugged on them until they gave way. In a whisper, the outfit fell to the ground. She removed her hand from the root of his cock to quickly untie the straps at her ankles. Slipping his hand under her arms he picked her up. She automatically wrapped her legs around his waist.

"Just the tip," he moaned as if he was in pain. Slowly, he hooked his left finger in the thong, followed it down her ass crack before he pulled it aside to expose her hot, wet pussy to his thick, long, questing cock. He grabbed the root of his dick to hold it still as she lowered herself onto it.

"Fuck," he groaned. It was as if her pussy was on fire. It was so damn hot. The way her soft, creamy walls felt as they gripped, massaged, and squeezed all around him made him pant for more. His grip tightened on her hips as he fought the urge to thrust into her. "That's enough," he said through clenched teeth.

Andreas wasn't the only one that was fighting the desire to give into the sensations that skin on skin was creating. She withdrew him from her body just to lower herself again, each time allowing him to penetrate her further. However, his strong hold on her hips limited her from taking too much of his length. She captured his mouth. Her kiss was deep and slow. She locked her ankles together and waited until she felt his grip relax. In one fluid movement, she slipped all the way down his dick until he was seated completely inside her.

"My God, what are you doing?" he groaned against her wet lips. When she began to grind her hips, Andreas was finished with asking questions. He turned and walked over to the closest wall. Only pausing to press her against it, he began fucking her fast at a punishing rate. Her moans and cries for him to slow down were lost on him. He was one tracked, one minded, and focused on pushing her, stretching her, to find more of the unexplainable feeling her body was giving him. He slowed down to enjoy the sticky, wetness of her juices that saturated his dick and collected in his hair and nuts. He rotated his hips before he bent his knees to grant him a better angle before he picked up the pace.

Calico tried to climb the wall, but there was no getting away from him. She hadn't taken into account all the activity they had indulged in all night long and that morning. He felt so damn good, but mixed in with the pleasure was also pain. She pushed his black hair out of his eyes. The intense expression in their blue depths made her walls tightened. He was gorgeous, manly, sexy, and dangerous. Unable to control herself, she licked his neck and tasted his salty sweat. He tilted his head, exposing more of it and his shoulder.

"Shit," he hissed from the sting of her biting him hard. He pushed her back against the wall. He pinned her with his narrowed gaze. She had a crazy, wild look in her gray eyes. He lowered his head to her breast, beginning to suckle. Suddenly, he sucked hard, and bit her nipple while he moved inside of her. Frustrated she pulled hard on his hair, until he let go.

"Do, you really want to do this, Coco?" he asked as he rotated his hips.

She leaned forward as if she was going to kiss him, instead she captured his bottom lips and sucked on it, hard. "I've always wanted to do that."

He touched his lip throbbing from the force of her mouth. He didn't know what had gotten into her. All of a sudden the game was no longer fun for him. The thought of treating her like all the other women he had been with was undesirable to him. She was different. From the beginning, she was and will always be different. She wasn't just a body, a willing pussy, or his bitch, she was... Andreas's mood changed and his kiss proved it. It was soft, lingering, and it melted her to the core. He carried her over to the bed. Still joined, he laid her back only to roll over on his side, taking her with him to face him. He reached down and rested her leg up upon his hip.

His kisses were so tender that she wanted to cry. Unlike the other times, his eyes focused upon hers as they looked at each other from behind hooded lids. Neither one knew how long they just kissed, touched, and whispered to one another before he began to thrust in her slowly. He held her gaze, allowing both of them not only to experience the pleasurable sensations firing off in their own bodies, but also the visible expressions of satisfaction. He covered her mouth with his to inhale her scream when her orgasm overtook her. A heartbeat later, he pulled out just in time for his cock to jump between their bodies as it sprayed it's hot cum on the front of her belly.

"Out of all the times, that was the *best*," she beamed like a little girl coming off an amusement ride.

Andreas laughed as he shook his head.

**

LaFaye stood by the door and checked his reflect. His had made sure that he was on point when he had gotten the call that he was going over. He wasn't too surprised. The man had taken to coming by whenever he needed a break from prying eyes or his wife. Although it was just usually drinks, him discussing his day, or asking LaFaye for advice, there were those rare times when he wanted a bit more before he strolled out of his apartment. He smiled at his reflection. He had gladly noticed that those rare times were becoming a lot more frequent at the end of his little visits. He knew that it was because of the pains he had taken to ensure his transformation was a natural one that made him look like a woman from a magazine. Of course, he still had to make sure he hid his dick from him whenever he was fucking him, but it was only a matter of him until he would have a nice tight pussy for him to enjoy.

"I don't know why you have to make me wait. Your punk ass was probably standing by the door," huffed Russell as he strolled past LaFaye.

He flashed Russell as toothy grin.

"Is that food I smell?"

"Yeah, I thought you could stay and eat," offered LaFaye.

"Nah, I can't stay," he responded, tossing himself down on the couch. His beady eyes examined the shapely man. He smiled at the fact that he was wear one of the outfits he had bought for him. It amazed him how a few operations were able to change LaFaye from the then, nappy headed, man with bad skin he had known while in prison, into the smoothed skinned, classy, natural formed woman in front of him.

LaFaye hid his hurt behind a laugh as he sat next to Russell. He knew that the asshole could be mean, but for some reason, he just couldn't stop hoping.

"So what do you want to talk about?" asked LaFaye.

"Can you believe that bitch?"

LaFaye paused as he tried to figure out who he was talking about. If he was referring to Wanda, he didn't recall her doing anything out of the norm. "Who are you talking about, Wanda?"

"Wanda," he spat. "Yeah, that cunt too, but I was talking about Calico."

LaFaye sat back in the chair.

"You know she works for me at the office. She walked around there like she was some saint, but the bitch ain't nothing but a whore. I can't stand the fact that she laying up with that Italian cock sucker. And yeah, Wanda, too. You saw the way she was acting like she was running things in the meeting. She shouldn't even be at the damn meetings. She ain't the *Don*, I am. I tell, you it's a shame you aren't a real woman," he mumbled, eyeing LaFaye full breasts. Without even asking, he reached out his hand and pulled down the plunging neckline, freeing one bouncy globe.

LaFaye let out a faint scream at the force he pinched his nipple. He was never gentle. It had always been that way with him. Even in prison when he would give LaFaye the signal to go out to their meeting place, Russell was always hard, like a grunting pig. LaFaye knew he could have other lovers, but Russell was his favorite.

"I thought we were going to talk?" LaFaye reminded him.

Sucking his teeth, he said, "I paid for those tits. Don't tell me those pills you're taking is turning you into bitch, too?"

"I was just making sure you were done talking, that's all," he reassured him as he leaned forward into his hand. He wasn't going to make the same foolish mistake that had gotten him a black eye when he had tried to kiss Russell. As for him paying for his chest, it was actually the same woman he couldn't stand that had paid for and had gotten him in with the plastic surgeon that had done all his work. However, he would never tell him that it had been Wanda.

"I just need to let off some steam. It won't be too much longer before I put them all in their place," he mumbled under his breath as he released his other breast. "Do you have those special underwear on under that skirt?" he questioned.

LaFaye had fashioned crotch-less underwear with the opening running down his ass to ensure that his male bits weren't seen by Russell, while his skirt was long enough to allow the ability of pleasuring himself secretly without Russell having to witness it. He would have liked to have to Russell to take a bath first, but once again, he wasn't a fool.

At LaFaye's nod Russell unzipped his pants. "Good. Come on then."

Chapter 7

Neither one of them could resist it no matter how hungry they were. It wasn't until his cell phone began to vibrate on the nightstand that he realized he was lying in his bed, still clothed with Calico. He snatched up the phone to stop the alert, but didn't read the text. He turned his head and stared out the large window at the tree outside his room. He had always loved that tree for many different reasons throughout his life.

As a kid, it was because of the bright orange, pink blossom. Then as a teen, it was because the branches of the tree were strong enough to support his weight so he could sneak himself out, or girls in. He frowned at the last fact. He decided he would have to have the tree cut back to ensure any of his kids didn't follow in his footsteps.

His train of thought caused him to turn his head again, this time to look at a still sleeping Calico. He reached over and pushed hair back from her face to stare at her. Even in the midst of slumber, she was beautiful. He wondered why a guy had never taken the time to see the woman that he was looking at now. Why they had never seen the woman he had met two years ago. For some reason he had seen the real her, and he never wanted to look away. He tried to recall something that his Grandmother had said when she spoke to him about why he was watching over Calico from a distance, but the more he tried, the further away the words became.

If he was honest, he had felt the rush of excitement when he had learned of Calico's involvement in bringing down Russell. Once he had gotten over his initial shock, his mind had gone into overdrive as it conjured up ways to use that twist of fate to bring her back into his life. After two years of fighting the urge to tip the scales of fate, fate had stepped in and placed her in his lap. Andreas didn't care if she was pregnant, or if Aunt Flo came knocking on the door tonight, there was no fuckin way she was going to get away from him this time. He didn't actually know what that meant. He didn't care if she would be his girlfriend, or wife just as long as she was here with him. The peace she brought him, her honesty, her strength, her wisdom, and whole other slew of emotions she stirred up in him that he couldn't even name was something he wasn't going to give up.

He smiled, slowly. "It only took one time, with the right person to change a man's life," he whispered, finally recalling his grandmother's words.

A soft curse left his lips as the cell started up again. Annoyed, he read the message which lead to him reading all the others that must have come through while he was knocked out cold.

"Coco, you need to get up baby," he ordered as he shook her. He smirked at her sleepy protest. Sitting up, he leaned over and bit her on her ass. That got the reaction he wanted and more when she punched him. "We have guests coming in about three hours," he explained.

She rubbed her stinging ass cheek while she sat up. "Business or just entertaining?"

Andreas's eyebrow went up at her comment. It was something in her tone that was different and boss like. "It's business. You can leave and come back later if you don't want to—"

"Why would I do that?" she questioned, cutting him off.

"I just wanted to give you the option since—"

"You just tell me if you need me to do anything, okay?"

He narrowed his eyes as he watched her stroll into the bathroom. He wanted to ask her what was up., But, he really didn't have the time to ponder on what was the cause in her sudden change? Him being a man, Andreas knew that just because the sex was good, and in their case great, didn't mean that your heart was in it. He had more reasons than just pussy to want Calico, but she had never expressed having any more than sex or their arrangement to be there. Besides, this wasn't a movie. He couldn't expect for her to be head over heels for him in less than 24 hours. She hadn't seen him in two years. It wasn't the same for her as it was for him. He hadn't been physically present, but he had been loving her from a distance.

Walking out of the room, he took the stairs two at a time. Quickly he went to the kitchen, opened the fridge, and pulled out enough meat for everyone. He shouted throughout the house until the short man that resembled the guy off of *Fantasy Island* entered the kitchen. He instructed him to season the meat, and prep the vegetables. Then he continued through the kitchen and down the hall to his Grandmother's suite. He decided it was better to take a bath in her room than in his with Calico to ensure he didn't get too distracted.

He reentered his room just in time to see her sitting on the trunk in just a black bra and lace black underwear, rubbing shea butter on her left thigh.

Lord have mercy, he prayed.

Calico looked up at the sound of the door opening. She smiled wickedly.

"We don't have the time for any other that," warned Andreas.

"What are you talking about?"

"Don't play dumb. I see that look in your eyes while you're undressing me."

"That isn't too hard when you're standing there in just a towel," she laughed. However, he was right about her look. She had never thought she would like a man with hair on his chest, but she had been proven her wrong. Maybe it was the fact that it was straight and not curly, and it was a thin layer, not thick and bushy. It was dark against his naturally tanned skin. His skin tone only made his deep blue eyes stand out even more.

"You got a call when you were out," she informed him, going back to her task. She had other things on her mind that made lusting after Andreas at the moment a bit overly tasking. She was worried about this meeting, wondering about the plan he was cooking up, worried that the fact that she wasn't actually doing what the DEA wanted her to do was going to bite her in the ass, not to mention the fact that she still had to do the club, then there was Andreas. What was she going to do after this chapter of hell was closed? The fact that he had done all those things for her without asking for nothing in return spoke volumes. The check after their night together could have been just an act of kindness, but everything afterwards was far and beyond what was called for.

Maybe, you were just that good? The voice in her head suggested in which Calico snorted in doubt.

Yeah, that was a stretch. So, the man has feeling for you, but can you?

She knew the question wasn't pertaining to if she could develop feeling for Andreas. That had already started to happen. No, her mind was asking if she could take on this type of life as a *Don's* woman? She knew she didn't have to worry about him protecting her, but all the other things that she was sure went along with it. What would happen when the DEA put him on their black list? She couldn't take losing him for life while he rotted away behind bars, or even worse, he was killed.

People die every day, Calico. Parents, friends leave for work, school, or to go to the store...or they lay down to sleep, and don't return. But that can't scare you. That can't keep you from loving, baby girl.

She sniffed and concentrated on rubbing the shea butter onto her arm as the voice of her Grandmother sprung up in her mind.

Andreas remained still as he leaned on the door frame of the walk in closet. He had been watching her lost in thought as he had gotten dressed. He could tell that she was crying. He started to speak only for her to do so at the same time. He nodded for her to go first, hoping that she was going to reveal what was wrong.

"Why doesn't the DEA come after you and the others?"

He bit his lip in frustration. She was hiding from him still. He ran his hands through his hair. "For years, we've been given a standing agreement with the powers on Capitol Hill. Believe it or not, many of my connections and customers came from behind the tall walls of those mansions. They happily turned a blind eye to the drugs, weapons, and prostitution just as long as it was within what they considered a normal limit, and it was done peacefully and from out of the eyes of the public masses. As long as it the poor and middle classes that are greatly affected, they didn't give a damn. Once and awhile, we'll stage a bust or two to make it seem as if the police force is putting the tax payer's dollars to good use, but in light of all the millions that we bring in every year, it's a good trade off," he explained as a matter of fact.

"So, the only reason there's an issue is because Russell is trying to change the rules? Other than that, they don't bother you?"

He was confused by the sound of hopefulness in her voice. "Yea. That's the way it's always been, and I don't see it changing any time soon."

"And what about hostile takeovers?" she asked as she began to get dressed in the floral short set she had placed on the bed. "You know, like you see in the movies. One mob boss wants a bigger piece of the pie, so there's guns blazing and stuff."

The drama in her voice had him laughing while he shook his head. "I'm sure that happens in other places," he waved his hand. "But not here, not in a long time. There's enough money for everyone. The lines have been lain, so why fuck with it? That's why things were created the way that they were so we all can watch each other's back. When the time comes to pass the torch, we still have to vote to make sure that the person will keep to the ways. Then if shit happens, because it does, like now, then we wipe that shit out as quickly as possible."

"So, you can see your kids carrying the torch in your name?"

He stiffened. Now, he knew what was going on. It didn't explain her tears earlier, but it still gave him an indication of what she had been thinking. The fact that she was asking these questions made the tempo of his heart sped up. She was considering staying with him.

"*Our* children can choose to be and do whatever they want. This is just their Daddy's job, nothing else," he said hoarsely. He was doing what he had heard one day while at a barber shop. The black preacher on the TV said to speak what you want into existence, and Andreas wanted the dark chocolate beauty that was standing across the room as she did her best to hide her feelings from him.

"I hope you know how to cook?" he announced, clapping his hands.

Calico chuckled. She was happy that he had changed the conversation. "Yes, I know how to cook.

"I would think so with all that ass," he teased, slapping it as he walked passed her towards the door.

He gave her a quick tour of the house on their way downstairs to the kitchen. It didn't take her long to fall in love with place. He strolled through the curved archway to enter the kitchen. If it wasn't for the gas burning gourmet stove, and the large marble topped island, she would have thought it was just another room. All of the other appliances were hidden behind chestnut colored cabinets.

"Here," he said, tossing her an apron. Quickly, he tied one around his waist.

"Why don't you have a cook?" she frowned.

"Nobody got money for that shit," he replied in a voice like Huey's grandfather off of the *Boondocks*, Mr. Freeman.

They laughed, teased, snacked, and argued while they cooked the stuffed pork chops, wild rice, and broccoli Florentine bisque soup.

"I have to start working on the club," she sighed.

He nodded. This had been her dream before he met her. He didn't want to hinder her in pursuing that. "I need you to not go to the club for the next three days. Can you work from here until then?"

"Yeah, I have to draw up my ideas and call around for prices. Why?" she questioned.

"Because Russell will be dead by then."

He answered her question as if he was telling her the time. There were no feelings in his tone at all. He had made the statement with so much confidence, too.

She swallowed hard. "Will that cause a problem with me and the DEA?"

"I don't see why it would," he replied glancing at her. "They will still get what they want; a name. As for him being six feet under versus being in a jail cell, I just saved them thousands. Does that bother you?" he inquired, untying the apron.

She shrugged. Her gaze flew to his face to find him frowning at her. She had forgotten how that pissed him off. "To be honest, I don't really know. There's that part of me that says fuck his nasty ass. The man is crazy, and hard, and doesn't give a damn about anyone or anything other than money and power. But then there's the other part of me that points out that he's still a living being. Although, he'll never change, he's still living...you know what I mean?" she asked, tilting her head.

Andreas walked over to her and pulled her into his arms. "Just as long as you never lose that other half that makes it hard for you to be completely cold when it comes to live, you'll be OK, but there also has to be balance. Some weeds need to be pulled up so the rest of the garden can grow," he pointed out.

He lowered his head to kiss her but froze at the sound of the front gate buzzer.

"Damn," she grunted.

Andreas tossed back his head in a fit of laughter. He picked up the remote to the flat screen that was mounted on the wall and turned it on. The image of the gate split into four tiny screens in black and white appeared on the TV.

"Flowers," she said in a high pitched voice.

"Don't get too excited," he chuckled as he pushed the buzzer and left her in the kitchen to finish setting the table.

Ten minutes later he returned with the tall Haitian she had seen at the club and three other men.

"Please tell him to take that ugly wig off," the tall man grunted.

Calico's eyes widened when the men that removed the dreadlock wig from his head was Chubby.

"You just jealous that my locs look better than yours," he laughed.

"Bullshit."

"Calico, this is Milky. You already know Chubby, and those two aren't worth naming," teased Andreas.

She set at the table and marveled at how they all laughed and joked during dinner. It was more like a party than an actual meeting. She listened to the stories that they told about one another, most of it embarrassing. She didn't know what she had expected, but it wasn't this. Finally, after clowning for a while after the meal was done, they got down to business.

"It went down just like you said it would happen. He called me over to get the ball rolling," said Chubby.

"I knew he would have to do something to flex his muscle. I'm just happy it was sooner than later," replied Andreas.

"I knew something was up when the guy you showed me started to move," stated Milky. "I thought he was never going to leave his girl's house. That's all the dude does is buy that fake ass gold from the flea market, smoke weed, eat, and fuck," he added.

"We got a few of our boys on him to see where he goes. When he goes to the lab, we'll know," stated one of the no names.

"You know if we move without Aldo's blessing, that could cause trouble," warned Milky. He was a *Don* also, but he wasn't that high on the pecking order.

"I'm not worried," shrugged Andreas.

"Of course, you aren't man cuz he's your Uncle, but I'm not family. Can I count on you?" pressed Milky.

"I'm going to have another talk with him," sighed Andreas.

"Then you better get to talkin'. It won't be long before all our ducks are in order. We should be ready to move in the next 24 hours," remarked Milky, pausing. "Are you going to try to absorb his territory into yours? The others might not like that, you know."

Andreas tilted his head to the side. "I could care less about expanding. I have more than enough as is. I probably would have let it all play out if it wasn't for other reasons." He saw all the eyes at the table shift over to Calico. "Yes, that *and* his outright disrespect. I think we all knew it was going to end this way."

"Well, you know Wanda is poised to reclaim it after he's dead," reported Chubby.

"Shit, she should have had it in the first place after her father was killed," the other no named man pointed out.

"I don't think she's going to let herself be cheated out of it this time. She's sided herself with the DEA and us. She doesn't give a damn what happens to Russell just as long as the fat fucker is gone," growled Chubby.

They all exchanged looks at the raw anger that was in his tone.

Never being the one to shy away, Milky lean forward, "Why...why you so mad, man? What's happened between you and him?"

Chubby stole a quick glance at Calico before he lowered his head in shame. "You met my little girl today, didn't you?" he asked. He looked at her. "I bet you think I'm a no good father for letting her get up on that stage in front of all those men, huh? You don't have to say it," he said, stopping her from speaking. "You know he had been fucking my little girl, and I didn't even know it? When I thought she was being tutored after school, he was fuckin her. Then when he got her pregnant, he took her to get an abortion. Here we all were wondering why she was so depressed? Why her grades were dropping, and her weight... shit, I even mentioned it to him, and he knew. The motherfucker knew all the time. That first week she started to dance, I would go to that club and beg LaFaye not to put my baby girl on that stage, but what could he do? He wasn't going to have Russell come after him. Just like I didn't say anything when I found out what had happened. Russell would have beaten me, or killed me. She's only seventeen. She just stays in the apartment. She can't bring herself to talk to us. She doesn't care anymore about herself, or anything because of the shame."

There was nothing that anyone at the table could say. They were all struck dumb by the revelation they had just heard.

That night neither one was in much of a mood for sex. Instead, they talked and watched the basketball game on TV in bed. Calico tried to remind herself what Andreas had said earlier, but now she felt nothing but rage which created a coldness in her chest for Russell. The man was truly a weed that need to be dug up and tossed into the fire to be burned.

**

"I would really appreciate it if you put that out," said Zita as she frowned at the cigarette.

"Oh yes, right," gulped Wanda. She bruised herself to put it out to keep anymore smoke from getting into the woman's face. She hadn't been thinking when she had lit up while she waited for Zita to show up at her beach home. Wanda had taken to staying there instead of remaining in the same house with Russell.

"I know it's your body, but you should seriously reconsider smoking," suggested Zita. She had known Wanda for years. She had always like the little girl, and the woman she had become. "I know why you've asked me here," stated Zita, cutting to the chase. She had plans later that evening, so she was pressed for time.

"I had no doubt that you would."

"You want me to talk to Aldo on your behalf in hopes of taking over after Russell is disposed of." Zita could see the look of shock on Wanda's face, but the she gave it to the woman. Her recovery was quick.

"I thought he was going to be hand over to the DEA?"

Zita shook her head. "No, I think things have gone far past that. The way Russell is now, not only would he turn on the people he has making that damn stuff, but he would turn State's evidence against everyone else, too. We would be crazy to give him over to the DEA?

Wanda nodded at the intelligence of the woman sitting before her.

"I would have thought this verdict would have please you, child. Russell being the one that had killed your father in the first place, and then bribing the three *Dons* to vote him in," revealed Zita.

This time, Wanda's expression didn't change. Zita tilted her head as she wondered if she had known about that all along. She opened her mouth to question her, but the figure approaching them at the table gave made her stop. She had seen the young man before when he had worked for Rush. He had the same hyper way about him that had made her question if the man was on drugs. Then she realized that he was just a smooth talker that thought that if he talked enough, he could convince a person to believe in whatever lies he was telling. She nodded and smiled her greeting at the young man.

"Rush, is there something wrong?" asked Wanda. She had no intention of introducing him to Zita no matter how hard he stared at the woman.

"I, I just came by to let you know that I didn't intend for my sister to get up with Andreas. I didn't even know that had liked each other," he swore.

Zita narrowed her eyes.

"Really? Well that's not what they said last night, and from the way things happened today, I think Calico has been doing a few things you don't know about," chuckled Wanda. She could tell that Rush was pissed over that last point she had just made.

"Well, I'm letting you know that I'm going to get her mind back on what I sent her there to do and not be fucking around with him," he promised.

"Why do you need to do that? The girl can have a little fun, *and* still get the information. As a matter of fact, her being with Dre may actually be in our favor," explained Wanda.

"Maybe, but I'm still going to talk to her," he pressed at which Wanda just shrugged.

"I don't know how you plan on doing that, but you tend have a way of making her obey. All I'm saying is if Dre gets pissed, I have nothing to do with it," warned Wanda.

Zita rubbed her chin in thought long after Rush had been swallowed up in the shadows of Wanda's home, leaving them alone again.

"What's wrong?"

"I'm just wondering why you have that weak, two faced man in your circle?" Questioned Zita.

"First off, when I marked him for the DEA I didn't know he was going to involve his sister. Yeah, I told them about Rush because I knew he would do whatever they said because he's scary as hell," she admitted at Zita's surprised expression.

Zita laughed. "I think you will do very well running things. You're very cunning, Wanda. I just hope all that plotting and scheming doesn't come back to bite you in the face," stated Zita, getting to her feet. "There's only two things though; 1. I want that motherfucker, Rush dealt with. 2. If you ever plot against Aldo or Andreas, I'll gut you in a special way to make sure see yourself bleed out before you take your last breath. Welcome to the *Don* hood."

Once again, Wanda gulped as she silently nodded. She had no doubt that Zita could back up what she just put down.

Chapter 8

Thankfully, the bright Miami sunlight brought a feeling of normalcy back into her life. Andreas was his regular laid back, flirty, handsome self as well. He was constantly on the phone talking in French, Creole, or in Italian as he handled his business. Calico didn't mind because she had work of her own to handle. She was on the internet looking up trendy clubs, fabrics, colors, furniture, and other key elements for inspiration. Andreas listened to her phone conversations. He shouldn't have been shocked that she knew what she was talking about. She was very professional in the way that she handled her business. Shocked was the wrong word. He was very impressed.

"Do you have a degree in interior design?"

"No," she replied, sheepishly. "I got my AA and one year towards my bachelor's in business, but I took a few classes in interior design."

"So you're self-taught, then. Can you take old furniture and revamp it?"

"Yeah, I can do that, too."

He looked at her in awe. She was full of surprises. He rolled his eyes at his cell.

Every time, he thought.

He was getting ready to work on getting some afternoon delight when it begun to ring. The name of the phone was like a bucket of cold water on his lust.

Now I don't have to call him, he acknowledged.

Calico went back to her working, think it was just another one of his calls.

"Come out to the beach home, *with* the girl."

Andreas groaned. If that was all his Uncle had to say, it was because he was saving it all for when they got there. An hour later, he led Calico through the backyard to the boat that had been sent for them. It wasn't until they had left the coast behind that she began to question where they were going.

"Do you see that land out there," he pointed. He waited until she nodded. "That's where we're going.

"But that's not a beach house. That's a freakin' tiny island," she shouted over the motor.

"Tomato, potato, that's his beach house."

The walk through a very unkempt yard brought them to a one level home that was at least 2100 square feet. The home looked as if it had been flown in from a Jamaican sugar plantation with its high columns, and wicker ceiling fans on the porch. Andreas punched in a code on the door and walked into the home. Polished cherry wood floors ran throughout the open plan styles home. She followed him as he strolled through the home to the wall of windows that had been pushed opened to the large patio and in ground pool out back.

"Aldo," shouted Andreas to get the attention of his Uncle. "What the hell?" he chuckled as he elbowed Calico.

"See it."

They both tried to keep straight faces at the scene before them. Aldo was having fun rubbing suntan lotion on the breasts of a girl that was in her twenties. He leaned over and kissed her before he acknowledged the two of them. He waved them over. Andreas turned to see a blonde stepping out of the pool. Her large breasts were barely contained within the top of her bright yellow bikini. Her body was fit and toned. As she got closer, he noticed the diamond belly ring that sparkled in the sun. She turned to the side and his eyebrows went up at the tattoo of a mermaid kissing a man that was inked stopping at her hip and starting just below her breast.

"I think that one is going to be too hard to handle," whispered Andreas.

Aldo glanced over his shoulder at the woman in question. "She always was and she always will be," he chuckled. He got to his feet. "And this precious queen here is…"

"Calico," she said as she extended her hand. The man was still handsome at his age. It was no wonder he had no problems getting the ladies.

"Your eyes are stunning. Do you know how you got them?" he inquired as he guided her over to the table under a thatch roof. The smell of the grill cooking filled the air.

Andreas fell in step while he listened to Aldo charm Calico. He kept walking toward the grill to have a look. His stomach was already crying out for the sausage, corn, and lobster tail that was sizzling on the racks. His body stiffened as a hand slid down his back. He crooked an eyebrow at the blonde standing next to him in a colorful, see through wrap and dark shades.

"That's some nice meat," she stated in a husky voice.

Andreas gazed over at his Uncle to find the man watching the two of them closely. He looked back at the woman. He knew she wasn't referring to what was on the grill.

"It does look good," he responded as respectfully as he could muster.

"I wonder if it will melt in my mouth."

Andreas blinked. He smiled, "Um, I like my women young, no disrespect."

"And black, I see. If you're crazy enough to do that, then you might be daring to try something with a lot more experience," she suggested. She saw the expression on his face change. This is what she wanted to see. She was tempted to take a step back due to the anger sparking in his eyes.

Calico glanced over her shoulder to investigate what had Aldo so focused. She started to her feet but his hand shot out to keep her in her seat. He shook his head to tell her to mind her business. He applied enough pressure to her arm to let her know he was serious.

"I don't give a fuck who you are, lady but understand this, you can either go back to get in the pool, or you can change your tone, because if you make the mistake of disrespecting her, I'll burn your damn tongue out," he sneered in a low voice to make sure it didn't carry.

The woman stared at him from behind her dark shades. "Well... well, it didn't take long for that chocolate pussy to get a grip on you, boy...but it can't be just that," she said taking a step back as he started to move towards her. He was mad. She smiled, snatching off her shades. He kept coming until he finally stumbled back as if it had been punched. He examined her in disbelief. He opened his mouth, but she waved her hands to stop him.

"I'm Zita," she spoke slowly.

He approached her slowly as he looked her up and down before he walked around her. He reached out his hand and lifted each of her ass cheeks.

"You never had an ass like this," he said in amazement.

"I never had a rack like this either. I mean, look at them," she offered only for him to stop her from revealing them.

"And the hair, and the tattoo, the belly ring... what da fuck? This isn't happening," he cried, pointing at her while he looked at Aldo to tell him it was a cruel joke.

"Come over here and have a seat before you faint, boy."

Andreas continued to size her up as he started to cry. Quickly, he pulled her into his arms, crushing her. She laughed and let her own tears flow.

"Oh, dear Lord," sighed Aldo as he rolled his eyes. "You two can do that over here, you know," he shouted.

"Who is she?" questioned Calico.

"If they can ever pry themselves apart, you'll hear it from the horse's big mouth," Aldo answered, loudly.

"Fine," shouted Zita. "You always have to be involved."

"That' right! How the hell I'm going to eavesdrop from way over here? I don't have *Dumbo* ears," exclaimed Aldo.

"So this the girl that had you in a hot sweat for the last two years, huh. Breathtaking eyes, pretty face, and hair, and one banging body," praised Zita.

"And it's all natural, too," snorted Aldo.

"Fuck you. You're just mad that I got the makeover and you didn't. Watch and see, he'll be getting some work done soon," she lamented as she tapped Andreas on his leg.

There was no denying that Zita was his grandmother.

"Nana, you did a lot more than getting a new ass and some tits," Andrea pointed out.

"Hey, watch it. Don't slip up when we're out there," she sighed, taking his hand. "That last treatment, when I went in to get the results, I had one of those moments when you look back over your life, you know. I told Jesus that if he let me live, I was going to *really* live with the time I had left. And the tests came back saying I was free of all the cancer. I was stage three, but it was all gone. I had them run the test again, and still nothing."

"But why did you leave me? Why didn't you tell me?" pressed Andreas.

"You know I couldn't just hang up the towel. And if I had stayed, they wouldn't have accepted you. They would have been coming to me questioning every decision you made. And you, you would have looked to me to *tell* you what to do," explained Zita. She waited to give him time to process her words.

"So who did your work?" he asked at last.

"Oh, I called Beau's dad, your Uncle in New York. You remember he got a new face when he went into the witness program. I got it all," she leaned over and dropped her voice, "I even got a new," she gestured between her legs. "You know... pussy."

Calico covered her mouth as she broke out in laughter while Andreas sat up in shock, and Aldo had a look of horror on his face.

"That explains why that young boy had his head up your ass for a month," said Aldo in disgust.

"I got the doctor's number. He can add a few more inches then you can make that sweet thing over there really cum," she remarked in a nastily tone.

Calico couldn't stop laughing at the brother and sister.

"Were you ever going to come back to me?" Andreas was hurt that she had him go through so much mourning her. But, he wasn't going to let that steal the joy he now felt having her back in the living. She wasn't the first one that had gone to such extremes in the attempt to have a normal life.

Zita kissed Andreas' cheek. "Silly boy, you know I was going to. It took me 8 months of surgery and recovery. Then I wanted to give you time to get settled and I had some fun. I'm very proud of you," she gushed. "And now that you have this little lady, I'll soon have babies to spoil. God, with that mixed skin tone, and hair, oh and I wonder what eye color they'll have?" she said as she clapped her hands.

"Well—"

"Oh, you two have time... just don't take too much time. This body is only newer on the outside. I'm still working with what God gave me on the inside," she warned, cutting Calico off.

"Now, let's get to it. Are you ready? Don't play coy. I know what you've been up to, and you should know you aren't the only one that's been move pieces on the chess board. There was no attack yesterday. I put that out to give you the fuel to justify the order," stated Aldo.

"Son of a bitch," laughed Andrea.

"Yes, she was. God rest her soul," he mumbled as he made the sign of the cross.

"I'm just waiting for the information to supply to the DEA," replied Andreas.

"That's why we called you. We have the names and an address," revealed Aldo. He reached into his shorts and produce a brown envelop. He pushed it over the table top toward Andrea.

"We'll meet you at the warehouse at ten. Milky will have Russell by then," said Zita, coldly. "I'll let you two get yourselves ready," she added, staring at Calico.

Chapter 8

Calico rode quietly in the Range Rover next to Andreas. The orange street lights reflected on the dark tinted windows as he sped down Interstate 95 toward the warehouse that Rush used to work. The fact that she knew she was on her way to witness the death of a man made her wanted to throw up. This was the world that she would be in if she chose to remain with Andreas. Although she wasn't going to be the one actually pulling the trigger, she had to be able to carry the weight of knowing. It was that information that she had to be able to deal with. She couldn't just pretend that this aspect of his life didn't exist as she walked around in her gated home.

He pulled into the open garage slowly. She watched through the side door window as the door closed behind them. Looking forward she counted the three cars that were already there with a few people talking outside of them. She recognized Milky, the two no named guys, Wanda, and a few other people she didn't know. Without a word, Andreas turned off the car and got out, leaving her in the car alone. Her eyes narrowed while she examined the scene playing out before her. She made a loud gasp when Andreas turned back to look at her. Slowly, he walked to the front of the car and told her to get out.

Calico's legs buckled as she got out of the car.

God, please don't make me have to watch, she prayed.

Andreas placed his hand on her lower back just as the back door to a black *Cadillac* opened. She saw everyone watching her as she walked over to the car, got inside, and closed the door behind her.

"I'm happy to see you made it," smiled Zita.

"I didn't think I had a choice."

"Oh, you have a choice. That's why you're here. I want you to understand your choice. My grandson is in love with you. When Aldo showed me the video he made of you two in the parking lot yesterday, and then today, when I disrespected you, I knew. But way back before then, when I found out he was helping you and you didn't even know it, I knew it even then. I asked him, you see, how he felt about you…why he even cared after a one nightstand? He said that he liked you, but that you were a good girl. He said that you were too good for him. He didn't think you would feel the same after you saw him for all he was…" She paused to knock hard on the car window.

At the sound of movement, Calico leaned forward. Her eyes widened at the sight of Russell fighting his captors as they wrestled to pull him out of the car in front. They dragged him over to the side of the window. He was close enough for her to see that he had put up one hell of a fight before they took him down.

"Now, that's Russell's wife. They've been together for over twenty years. Yea, she hates him because he's one nasty SOB, but there has to be some morsel of love left for him. However, she's willing to let him die. What I'm saying is that in this life, a woman has to have a hardness about her to do what needs to be done. She has to have her man's back. Now, if her man is a good one, like Andreas, and my husband was, she won't have to dirty herself with this side of the business, but she has to still *love* her man in spite of the monster he has to be. When you get back home, if you can still find Andreas attractive, if you can still laugh, kiss him, make love to him, and enjoy it, then you can be his woman."

With that said, she tapped again on the window.

**

Andreas walked away from the car as the two men dragged Russell around the corner. Swiftly, he pulled his leather gloves from his jeans pocket. He waited until they had placed Russell on the large piece of plastic they had already prepared. He glanced over at Aldo before her took the gun that had been handed to him.

"Chubby," he called.

The two of them exchanged a silent message before the man smiled and walked over to Andreas. Chubby took the gun in his gloved hand, strolled over to stand in front of Russell, and paused. His brown eyes bore into Russell's pleading ones as he cocked the gun.

**

Calico jumped at the sound of gun shots.

Three…four…five, she counted mentally before there was silence.

She felt drained as she got back into the vehicle with Andreas. What does a person say after an event like that? Were they clean shots? Did he suffer? Do you want to get a milkshake at *McDonalds*?

She had been so lost in thought that it took Andreas opening her car door to realize they were back at his place.

He waited until they were on the stairs to speak.

"You can leave."

His voice was so low that she doubted she heard him. Spinning around, she looked at him.

"You can go, Calico. You can take one of the cars. You don't have to stay," he swallowed. He preferred for her to leave now. He wouldn't be able stand her treating him coldly, or making excuse for him not to touch her. Obviously, the fantasy he had been playing for the last two years, and the last three days had finally come to an end.

It was the first time since getting back in the SUV with him, that she had really looked at him. Her eyes widened. He hadn't grown horns. He didn't look twisted or deformed. He still sounded the same, and his presence still produced the same tingle in the pit of her stomach as before.

"Are you kicking me out? I'll get my stuff—"

"No," he shouted, grabbing her hand to stop her. Touching her hand to his chest, "I don't want you to go. I want to lock you in my room to keep you from going. I want to fall asleep in you so that when I wake up in the morning, I can make love to you all over again," he confessed, in a hoarse voice. "Listen," he continued. "I was asked the question, why I did those things? I know it sounds crazy, but I love you, Coco. After that night, I couldn't stop thinking about you. You've never *seen* me, but I was always there for you. But because of this, I robbed myself of the joy of being with you. I can't do what Zita has done, so before you go any further, you need to be sure that *I'm* what you want. I don't want to do the I want you today, then I hate you tomorrow, shit."

His heartbeat thundered against her open palm. He was nervous. That's when she felt it. The creamy fluid dripping to stain her panties as it got her pussy ready for him. She saw the hurt in his blue eyes as she withdrew her hand from his. Slowly, she took hold of her shirt and lifted it over her head followed by her bra. She felt his warm breath against her skin as he exhaled. Taking hold of his face, she began to kiss him deeply, slowly.

Andreas arms snaked around her waist as he lifted her into his arms. He walked down the hallway with determination to do exactly what he had promised.

Chapter 9

"Will somebody stick something in that queen's mouth?" Groaned Zita.

"This is a wake," he brother reminded her.

"Yes, I know that, but is all that screaming really needed?"

Andreas glanced across the room. The second LaFaye had entered the room he had been in rare form. He hadn't moved from his spot in front of the large photo of Russell. The fact that it was a private wake for the *Don's*, their families, and all of the associates at Wanda's beach house didn't change the fact he was creating a scene. He was torn between going to comfort LaFaye or going over to where Calico was standing. He knew it was only a matter of time before Rush made his move to talk to her.

"Go over there and shut him up, please," mumbled Aldo as he headed for the front of the table to handle the business of officially entrusting Wanda the district that was once her father's and then Russell's.

**

"I bet you think you're the shit now, huh? All I can say is you better be happy that this shit played out alright," he grunted.

Calico had been wondering when he was going to make his way over. She had been waiting for him.

"Why should I have been worried about things not working out?" she asked sweetly.

He regarded her strangely. "Your black ass was on the line, too. If I went down, you would have gone with me. So, I was wondering if you could ask—"

"No," she said, cutting him off. "I wouldn't have gone down with you seeing how you lied when you said you had given me money, but you already knew that, right?"

"Whatever. Shit, if I had known you had fucked him that night, I would have asked his ass for a bonus," he chuckled. "But anyway," he continued as he reached out his hand to pull her closer.

Calico jerked away. "I'm not asking Andreas nothing for you," she spat.

His narrowed his eyes. "Damn, his dick must be something else cuz it got you hallucinating that you're the shit. You wouldn't even be here if it wasn't for me."

Calico nodded. "You're right, for once. I would have never met Andreas if it wasn't for your scheming, and I wouldn't have gotten back with his if you hadn't sold me out, but I don't give two shits about you or helping you."

Rush took a step towards her, but froze at the loud scream. They both turned to see LaFaye push Andreas away before he fumbled with his purse. With shaking hands, he pulled out a gun and began waving it in the air.

"Don't you do it! Don't you fucking do it," he screamed, pointing the gun at Aldo.

Aldo took a seat as he pinned LaFaye with his steely blue gaze.

"Calm down, everybody," warned Andreas.

"You shut the hell up," cried LaFaye. "Or I'll shoot you first, but not before I pop a cap in your thirsty ass. Yeah, I'm talking about you," he stated as he trained his gun on Wanda. "All of this," he waved at himself, "I did it for Russell. You said you would help me. You promised me that Russell would be alright. You said that after he spill the tea, that he would be put into a program with a new identity. That he would walk away from this shit, and I could be there to pick up the pieces, but you fuckin lied bitch. You let him kill him! And for what?! So you can be called *Don*? So you can run things? Who did it?" he shouted. "Was it you, bitch?" he took a step towards Wanda. "Or was it you?" he asked, stepping to the side to swinging the gun on Andreas.

Andreas fought the urge to not look at Calico. He could see her moving slowly through the stun crowd towards LaFaye. He knew he had to choose to either close the gap between him and LaFaye which would cause him to shoot him in the chest, or run the risk of Calico getting hurt trying to do whatever she was planning. He closed his eyes at the sound of her voice. His heart stopped as he turned his head to glance at her.

"It wasn't Andreas that did it."

LaFaye blinked the stinging mascara out of his eyes in an attempt to clear his vision.

"I was there. I saw him. He was all beaten up, but Andreas didn't kill him," said Calico in an emotional voice. "You had said you were helping for love. I didn't know you meant him."

"He wanted your skinny ass, too," revealed LaFaye in a nasty tone. "But I know you didn't want him. I know you didn't have anything to do with this. Just tell me who did it?"

Calico prayed that she wasn't going to get another man killed, but she needed him to come closer.

"It was Rush." She saw the disbelief in LaFaye's face. She glanced back over her shoulder to see her brother starting to shake, still standing where she had left him.

"Bullshit! You're just saying that because it was Dre," replied LaFaye as he began turning back to Andreas.

"No, it was Rush. He did it because Wanda had promised him something just like she had promised you. I don't know what it was, but I swear that he killed Russell," she insisted.

Quickly, LaFaye waved the gun at Andreas, commanding him to get in front of him.

"Everybody, get back. Move at out my way," he ordered as he made his way through the crowd towards Rush whom looked like a deer caught in a pair of headlights.

Andreas tried his best to make his way over to her side, but the crowded pushed him in the opposite direction. He could tell that she was up to something over the fact that she was the only one still calm, and she hadn't moved from where she had been standing, which was along the path of LaFaye. He leaned to the side and that's when he caught a glimpse of what she had hidden behind her back. It was small and bright neon colored. He started to shove people out of his way after he realized what she was planning to do. However, it was too late. It felt as if the air had been crushed out of his lungs as he watched her raise her hand. Next came the light blue flash of electricity as it danced along the three cords that was propelled from the device to stick into the side of LaFaye's body. Followed by the loud shot from the gun that was caused by his body seizing up from the currents that flowed through his body, rendering him a flopping heap on the ground.

A few people ran to see where Rush had been hit while others surrounded LaFaye, taking the gun from his numb hands. Andreas didn't give a damn about anyone other than Calico. He grabbed her and began to shake her violently as his fear, anger, and relief mixed to overtake him.

"Are you fuckin crazy? He could have killed you. You could be dead," he snarled. Then I his next breath, "Oh, my God, Coco," he whispered, crushing her in his embrace.

Rush stood up in pain, holding his arm where he had been hit. His looked up to lock eyes with his sister where she hugging Andrea with her head on his chest. Her gray cold, expressionless eyes bore into his brown ones, sending a chill down his spine. There was no questioning the silent message she was sending him. It was obvious that she had been prepared to sacrifice him if it meant saving Andreas. Whatever love she had had for him was minimal if any now.

Zita waved Wanda over to where she had been standing behind Aldo.

"I think the young man had been dealt with just fine. If you chose to keep him in you ranks, that's up to you," she said coldly. She had known that Wanda was a cunning bitch, but she had no idea to the degrees the woman had gone to gain the seat she was now in. She waited until Wanda left to see to the handling of LaFaye.

"I hope the poor thing doesn't turn up in a canal somewhere," she mumbled.

Her brother cocked a questioning brow at her.

"Well, it's obvious he was being played. It was more grief than anything," she pointed out.

Quickly, he waved his hand, summoning someone over. He whispered in the man's ear, then sent him quickly on his way. He looked at his sister and shook his head at the beaming smile she flashed him as a thank you for making sure LaFaye didn't meet an untimely end.

"That was some shit," grunted Aldo as he gestured his head toward Andreas and Calico. "She was going to make sure nothing happened to Andreas. I think she's just as crazy over him as you are," he chuckled, tapping her on her arm. "Oh, don't be like that. You're not being replaced. He still loves you, and hey... soon they'll be babies for you to spoil," he added, trying to cheer her up.

"Oh, yes! The babies," Zita began to clap.

EPILOGUE

Seven months later...

Calico opened one eye to peek at Andreas to make sure he was still asleep. Slowly, she moved like a soldier as she crept out of bed. She didn't want to wake him until she was done. Quickly, she tiptoed to the bathroom and closed the door softly behind her. She had done this so many times the previous months with no luck, she didn't want to get him excited before she knew for sure. With shaking hands, she dug the box out of the dirty clothes basket. The step for testing for pregnancy had been committed to memory by now due to the many failed readings. She still had a week and a half to go until her period started again for this month, but she just felt this time would she would get the result they both wanted.

With sure hands after peeing on the stick, she set the test flat as the instruction stated. She felt as if she was going to go blind at the intensity of her glare as she willed the testing process to go faster, so she turned to face the wall as she waited. Unable to count the specks of light brown clay in the paint any longer, she closed her eyes, turned back around to the bathroom counter, and with her hand on her chest, she opened her eyes. Tears instantly sprang to her eyes at the sight of the digital reading that said positive. According to the reader, she was 3 weeks along. Her body rocked with emotion as she did her best to stifle her sobs.

She didn't know how long she stood there staring at the test in her hand. Glancing at the closed bathroom door, she took a picture. Quickly, she sent it in a text to Andreas, Aldo, and Zita. Then she waited. A few seconds later, her phone started to vibrate. She had to hold the phone from her ear due to the loud screams that Zita was making.

"Oh my God, yess!! What did Andreas say? No, don't tell me. I'm on my way. I—"

"Calico!!!" roared Andreas at the top of his lungs.

She could hear him stumbling and knocking things down in the room.

"Oh, I can hear him," giggled Zita.

"He got the same text as you. See you later."

She had just hung up when he came crashing through the door. He was panting as he walked slowly into the bathroom. She couldn't help but laugh at his dumbfounded expression.

"It's not a joke?" he demanded to know.

She held up the test for him to see.

He narrowed his eyes as he read the results. Then they widened into two blue pools when it hit him.

"A baby? We're going to have a baby. Well actually it's coming out of your...but you and me, together are having a baby," he said in amazement.

"Yes."

"I knew it! I knew it was only a matter of time before one of my swimmers made it," he beamed. "Yes! Fuckin' yes," he shouted as he picked her up. "I love you," he smiled as he kissed her.

"Zita is on her way," she laughed.

"Oh Lord," he laughed happily. He knew that they would be partying for days. He picked her up and carried her back into the bedroom. Getting serious, "I'll help you all I can with your business, but if you have to turn some jobs away, you have to put the baby first. So will you marry me now? No correction, you're *going* to marry me. I've been hinting at it for a while. You don't seem to realize that I'm not going anywhere, and neither are you. I won't wait any longer," he said, waving his hand when she opened her mouth. "Listen, you will *not* be walking around here carrying my baby and not have my name."

Calico scanned his handsome face. He had done everything to prove to her that he loved her while he waited for her to return the same level of intensity as him. He wanted more, but she had been the one dragging her feet. Even with getting on board with the idea of trying for a baby, she still had a piece of her that she still held back. It pained her to admit it, but it was true.

"You don't even have a ring."

He hopped out the bed, marched to the closet to disappear inside. A few seconds later, he reappeared with a large black box. Taking a deep breath, he opened it. He watched her face closely in hopes that he had done a good job in picking out the ring. If the tears streaming down her cheeks were any indication, he had done good.

"Do you like it? Because I heard pregnant women cry a lot?"

"Hush up and put it on my finger," she chuckled.

Taking the large ruby and diamond from the box, he slipped it onto her finger.

Caressing her face, "I know you have the ring, but more important, you have my heart, Coco," he said.

You can't be scared. What you're holding on to…it can't keep you from loving, baby girl, the voice of her Grandma whispered in her mind.

At the moment, Andreas didn't know what was happening. He was looking at Calico, but it wasn't her. It was someone different. A person he had only dreamt of seeing that was shining brightly in her large almond shaped gray eyes. It was if he could peer into her heart, she was so opened to him. He glanced at his hand as she placed it against her heart.

"I love you, Andreas."

With each crisp pronounced word she spoke, he felt the last chains that had kept her from loving him completely fell away. No more hiding. No more pretending. The woman he had been waiting on for over two years, was finally his, at last.

THE END

Thanx so much for reading!

Please make sure to leave a review on Amazon and Good Reads.

Also, don't forget to like me on my Facebook pages

https://www.facebook.com/SapphireIRRomanceFanPg/ and https://www.facebook.com/profile.php?id=100004513637903 and also on Instagram: *@ChristineSapphireGray*

Looking for a publishing home?

Royalty Publishing House, Where the Royals reside, is accepting submissions for writers in the urban fiction genre. If you're interested, submit the first 3-4 chapters with your synopsis to submissions@royaltypublishinghouse.com.
Check out our website for more information: www.royaltypublishinghouse.com.

Be sure to LIKE our Royalty Publishing House page on Facebook

CPSIA information can be obtained
at www.ICGtesting.com
Printed in the USA
LVOW04s1509220416

484887LV00020B/619/P